And Then
Brecke
Breckenridge, Donald
And then

$16.95
ocn967919372

First edition.

WITHDRAWN

Donald Breckenridge

AND THEN

Black Sparrow Books

David R. Godine, Publisher

BOSTON

This is
A Black Sparrow Book
Published in 2017 by
DAVID R. GODINE, PUBLISHER
Post Office Box 450
Jaffrey, New Hampshire 03452
www.blacksparrowbooks.com

Copyright © 2017 by Donald Breckenridge
Introduction copyright © 2017 by Douglas Glover

Cover art copyright © 2017 by Daniel Martin
www.danielmartin.nl

All rights reserved. No part of this book may be used or reproduced in any
manner whatsoever without written permission from the publisher, except
in the case of brief quotations embodied in critical articles and reviews.
For information contact Permissions, David R. Godine, Publisher,
15 Court Square, Suite 320, Boston, Massachusetts 03452.

LIBRARY OF CONGRESS CATALOGING-IN-PUBLICATION DATA
Names: Breckenridge, Donald, author.
Title: And then / by Donald Breckenridge.
Description: Jaffrey, New Hampshire : Black Sparrow Books, 2017.
Identifiers: LCCN 2016052960 | ISBN 9781574232295 (acid-free paper)
Classification: LCC PS3552.R3619 A85 2017 | DDC 813/.54—dc23
LC record available at https://lccn.loc.gov/2016052960

First edition, 2017
Printed in the United States of America

This book is for my father.

A headache after having drunk too much. Life is not a flower. Shit is. The ragout of orangutan of Rangoon. Rangoon makes the taste of orangutan ragout distasteful. I have burning regrets when, sometimes, I realize that I have tied myself down, that I have bound my hands, put leaden chains on my feet. To be free, to walk, to run, not to crawl anymore.

I have the key to happiness: remember, be profoundly, profoundly, totally conscious that you are. I myself, sorry to say, hardly ever use this key. I keep losing it.

EUGENE IONESCO
from *Present Past Past Present*
Translated from the French by Helen R. Lane

Introduction

DOUGLAS GLOVER

> We walk about, amid the destinies of our world-existence, encom-
> passed by dim but ever present Memories of a Destiny more vast—
> very distant in the bygone time, and infinitely awful.
>
> POE, *Eureka*

Donald Breckenridge is a pointillist, constructing scene after
scene with precise details of dialogue and gesture, each tiny in
itself, possibly mundane, but accumulating astonishing power
and bleak complexity. His language is matter of fact, the unsentimental plain style used subtly and flexibly, the only apparent
artfulness is in the unconventional punctuation and, sometimes,
the way the dialogue breaks up the narrative sentences. His
settings are Carverish, bleak and constrained; his characters
are the stubborn, alienated authors of their own melancholy
fates; they persist in a panoply of failed habits and attitudes,
gestures of a wounded self they refuse to give up because it
is theirs, a refusal that is by turns defiant, sordid, heroic, gro-
tesque, and tragic.

But this novel's triumph is in its rich architecture, its sur-
prising splicing of genre and quotation, its skillfully fractured
chronology, and the deft juxtaposition of alternating story lines.
The result of this combinatorial panache is to create an arena
of systemic implication, in which the sum is greater than the
parts. Nothing here is what you expect; in fact, some of this
text is nearly indescribable in terms of genre and form. What

9

Introduction

do you call a piece of fiction that is a narrative transcription of a real movie that is itself a fiction? Answer: Don't even try. It's a logical wormhole. It will turn your brain inside-out like a sock.

I will elucidate: *And Then* is, like most novels, a story about a character. Let's say a nondescript loser robs a mom and pop store in some out of the way town and gives the money to his girlfriend so she can escape the mean and derelict provincial life she is destined for. She heads to New York with the cash, finds an apartment share, has a love affair with a photographer, but the police (somewhere) are after her and she falls among bad companions, under the sign of hard drugs, who love her for her money. When that stake runs out, so does her string and she disappears, probably dead, floating in the river.

But Breckenridge, the symphonic composer, takes this narrative theme, his melody, as it were, and works elaborate magic upon it by adding five further structural elements.

1) A second, parallel plot involving a young male student who, a dozen years later, agrees to cat sit for one of his professors away on sabbatical. In the apartment he discovers the photograph of a beautiful woman, his professor's mysterious former lover and/or roommate, a woman who simply disappeared. The student obsesses on the woman in the photograph, he becomes a sleuth, collecting stray bits of information about her. He finally tracks down the photographer who took the picture. But no one knows what became of her.

These two plots, the young woman plot and the student plot leapfrog each other in the text, fragmented, uncanny. At a certain point the young woman, apparently waking from a drug stupor (only she is dead), finds her way back to the apartment, ascending the stairs just as the young student is descending. At the climactic moment, he feels her ghost passing through him.

2) Cut between the fragmentary paragraphs of the two fictional plots, Breckenridge inserts a brutal, sad memoir of his father dying: stark and beautiful and full of our common human-

Introduction

ity; pity, love, kindness, stubbornness, squalor and valor. Here again there are two narratives: one works back and forth over the story of a life, two lives, father and son, and the father's declining days; the other, more mysterious, follows Breckenridge to a diner, the subway, the train station. We get detailed accounts of conversations with the diner owner. We oscillate between donuts and staph infections, but by the genius of construction and understatement, horror and hopelessness accumulate. The word "love" isn't thrown around, but the son patiently bandaging dabbing medication on those awful sores tells you more than words. You are fascinated, cannot turn away.

Curiously, embedded in the memoir we find a scene in which Breckenridge tells his father about the suicide of a woman who lived in an apartment above him and how, he is sure, that one day he encountered her ghost in the stairwell. (The reader himself encounters a *frisson* of what Nabokov's fictional poet John Shade calls combinatorial delight.)

3) An epigraph from Ionesco's *Present Past Past Present,* an important influence for Breckenridge who takes epigraphs for all his novels from this text. The passage presents a character unfree, chained down, but conscious that he has the key to freedom, which he hardly ever uses.

4) An overture, or introductory passage, that consists of a prose transcription/narrative summary of Jean Rouch's film *Gare du Nord* (1965, one of six short films by leading New Wave directors under the title *Paris Vu Par*). The film splits into two parts. The first follows a young married couple quarreling over the dissolution of their relationship; they are tired of each other, disappointed in their mistakes, tired of their lives. In the second half of the film, the wife meets a handsome brooding fellow who offers transcendence, offers her the chance to run away to a life of adventure. But she's too bourgeois, timid, polite to take him up. His response is to climb the bars of a railway bridge and jump to his death.

Introduction

But what is going on? A novel disguised as a summary of a film? A quotation, as it were? A meta-commentary, or a work of art based on a work of art or in dialogue with a work of art? And the story itself is iconic, presenting the enormous ennui of modern life in the pressure cooker of a young marriage. But then the young man in the suit offers liberation. Is he a con, is he the devil, is he an angel? And the girl can't contemplate running away from the life that is grinding her down. She hurries back into the trap. She doesn't trust freedom—well who would trust a man you had just met, who talks crazily about adventure, who looks too good in that suit? What is she going to do now? The message loop Breckenridge creates is convoluted and mysterious and yet firmly within a novel-writing tradition starting with Cervantes who, after all, wrote a great novel about a man trying to imitate another book.

5) But, even more curiously, embedded in the memoir we also find a few paragraphs in italics quoted from Théophile Gautier's romantic horror story "The Tourist" (originally published as "Arria Marcella: A Souvenir of Pompeii" in 1852), a ghost story of sorts, in which a young traveler becomes obsessed with a woman's figure preserved in the ash of Pompeii only to find himself translated that night to ancient Pompeii where he falls in love with the very woman. The story has the air of Hawthorne's "Young Goodman Brown" or Keats's "La Belle Dame Sans Merci." The young traveler, sent back to his own time without the ghostly lover, never falls in love again, never fully engages with life.

And I awoke and found me here,
On the cold hill's side.

And Then is beautiful, artful, an elaborated system of repetitions, motifs and juxtaposed narratives. Without wishing to be reductive, one can say that the three ghost stories relate to

Introduction

the theme of co-presence of temporal periods signaled in the Ionesco quotation, the way the past haunts existence. And they are balanced with three stories of characters who cannot change their behavior when change is the only way to redeem themselves (the Paris girl who cannot leave her job and marriage, the girl who runs away to New York with her stash, and Breckenridge's father who cannot get himself the treatment that would save his life). And these in turn are refracted in three observer stories: the Brooklyn student who falls in love with the photo of a missing woman, the youthful traveler in Gautier's horror story, and Breckenridge watching his father die.

And Then is a contemporary ghost story, full of horror, unremitting melancholy, heir to the romantics, to Gautier and to Poe (yet also, stubbornly unsentimental, in effect, reminiscent of the Nouveau Roman), a vastly literate work, engaged in its own conversation with the bookish past. Everything here is doubled and redoubled, echoed, mirrored, and reflected, and the dead do not die. The dead turn into ghosts or memories or words on the page, all of which are the same perhaps, at least in a book. And the effect in this novel is to create a mysterious intimation of a larger reference, a world beyond the book, a teeming yet insensible world that is yet no consolation.

And Then

The film begins with a panoramic shot of the skyline above the 10th Arrondissement in Paris and is accompanied by the drone of jackhammers. The camera pans the horizontal jib of a large red crane suspended above a construction site then lingers on a young woman watering the flower box on a narrow windowsill overlooking the site. The interior scene opens with the young woman, attractive with shoulder length dark hair and wearing a yellow bathrobe, having breakfast with her husband who is dressed in orange pajamas. The husband is heavyset with tousled hair. He has the gruff demeanor of someone who did not get enough sleep. Breakfast consists of soft-boiled eggs, a baguette with butter and two bowls of black coffee. Their conversation is warm while recounting a weekend outing with friends, although he yawns through some of his lines, then grows contentious as they discuss the grind of the workweek. She wants to know why he thinks her desire to travel is so ridiculous. He says that it isn't ridiculous. She wants to know why he thinks her fantasies about escaping their everyday existence are so unrealistic. He assures her that there is nothing ridiculous or unrealistic about wanting to travel then adds that millions of young married couples around the world have found themselves working for meager salaries at entry-level positions in large corporations while living in small apartments. She reproaches him for what she perceives to be his condescending attitude then insists that they are trapped in a tiny, claustrophobic apartment in a dull part of the city, which is clearly ruining her life and destroying whatever chances she has of ever being happy. He is visibly annoyed by her proclamations. Their morning routine is poisoned by festering resentments as an alternating volley of diminished expectations begins in earnest. They move through the apartment exchanging insults. The casual resignation the actors employ while delivering their lines conveys the impression that the melodramatics on display are as much a part of the couple's daily routine as brushing their hair and teeth every morning before leaving for work. While shaving, the husband inquires, over the muffled drone of jackhammers from the nearby construction site, as to why he is entirely to blame for their current financial predicament. She sarcastically compares the crane looming outside their bedroom window to the Eiffel Tower. While stepping into a knee length skirt, the wife declares, that this passionless marriage is the ultimate source of her unhappiness. Hadn't she realized exactly what she was getting into before they married? What an ungrateful oaf she has had the misfortune of marrying—lazy, unlucky, a real slob. If he had known she was this shrill and superficial he would have never married her. She says this stifling middle class existence, having to live in a tiny apartment and her horrible position in an airless office are to blame for making her shrill and miserable. He says she has never been interested in resolving their conflicts, and yes, her unrealistic expectations feed a boundless narcissism, this constant fighting is nothing more than a selfish and destructive form of entertainment. The future looks grim, and she is now running late for a job she despises. While buttoning up her blouse she tells him they are finished. And how, the husband demands, is he to blame for that. She slaps him, after making the bed, and then walks out. The husband follows her out the front door and down the hall where he is willing to give up a little ground—you've blown this out of proportion but maybe we

And Then

have taken things too far. She refuses to reconcile and leaves him standing before the cage-like lift, repeatedly calling after her, as she descends through the building. The splice leading into the second part of Jean Rouch's short film, *Gare du Nord*, is hidden in darkness. She passes quickly through the lobby and into a Parisian spring morning circa '64. The 16-millimeter camera follows over her left shoulder as the morning sun highlights the dark green velvet ribbon in her auburn hair. The sound of her heels moving rapidly along the pavement accompanied by passing traffic. While crossing the street she is nearly hit by a car. A tall man in a black suit appears and apologizes for almost running her down. She is going to be very late for work. Can he give her a lift? She politely refuses. The man abandons his sports car in the intersection and follows her up the street. He is a handsome, Belmondo-type, with the somber demeanor of an undertaker or a down on his luck aristocrat. Although she says she has no time to talk, she engages him in an earnest conversation while walking up the street. The man says modern society has driven him to despair and claims to be seriously contemplating suicide. His confession doesn't shock her. He presents her with a highly implausible invitation—run away with me and we will live an extraordinary life of adventure, a life of unlimited love and endless freedom. He insists that they will never worry about money or be dragged down by the banalities of everyday existence. She is bemused by his offer and inquires as to how such a life with him would be possible. He quietly assures her that his family possesses vast wealth—serenely adding that having a lot of money is meaningless when you don't have someone to share your life with. Fleeting temptation crosses her expression before she politely refuses. When she claims they don't even know each other it's implied that anyone this impulsive is clearly unstable, yet she confesses her desire to travel, then relates her fantasy of just getting on a plane someday to fly away and begin again somewhere else as another person. They are walking along an overpass, with the sound of a commuter train rushing below, as the man tries to convince her to run away with him. She simply cannot. And now he is seriously threatening to kill himself at the count of ten if she doesn't accompany him. She apologizes for saying no, and begs him to stop, because what he wants from her is impossible. They continue walking as he calmly counts up to nine. At ten he climbs the railing of the overpass. She pleads with him to stop as he jumps to his death. The long distance shot of the screaming woman pulls back to reveal a motionless body lying face-up on the tracks. A loud train-whistle echoes her screams as the film ends.

Suzanne was sitting beside John in his VW, "All I want to do," with a six-pack nestled between her sandaled feet, "is get out of here." Three shirtless boys rode their bikes through the empty parking lot as alternating smells of honeysuckle and motor oil trailed into the open windows. "The weekend totals," John leaned over and removed a cold can from the bag, "counting Friday," pulled off the top, "if I don't make that deposit on Saturday morning," and flicked it out the window, "we're talking about ten grand." John was thirty-one, "Probably a bit more," with an unhappy wife, "if you count the petty cash," two-year-old son and a faltering mortgage. Suzanne was twenty-one, "Wow," and living with her grandparents again, "that's a lot of money," in the house she grew up in. "I was happy just to come back from Vietnam," John was born and raised in Cleveland, "in one piece," after dropping out of college he drifted down to Virginia Beach, "but if this is it," and stalled there, "I'm positively screwed." Suzanne relished his attention, "It can't be that bad," she had never met anyone like him. John flirted with all of the pretty cashiers, "I wish I knew you in my prime," and most of the young women who shopped in the supermarket, "we would've raised some serious hell together," but Suzanne was

And Then

his favorite. John never reprimanded Suzanne for always being late or when her drawer was short—it was usually five dollars under—he never commented on her frequent arguments with customers or for calling in sick most Saturdays. Suzanne hated her job, "Where would you go with ten grand?" John was trying to convince her, "We wouldn't need that much money in the Keys," they were trapped in the same cage, "way down in Big Pine." She noted the green pine tree air-freshener hanging from the rearview mirror, "There are way too many rednecks in Florida," then took a sip of beer before adding, "my idiot uncle lives in Jacksonville." John scored a lid of grass from a stock boy on Friday, "I still have some Army friends down in the Keys," after Suzanne promised to hang out with him after work on Sunday, "running charter boats." Moths had multiplied around the overhead lights. He suspected she wasn't paying attention, "Where would you go with ten grand?" With a smirk, "Where am I gonna get ten grand?" "Okay," John took a sip of beer, "half," wiped his mouth with the back of his left hand, "Where would you go with five grand?" Suzanne turned to him and said, "New York City." A police car pulled into the parking lot. "Maybe we should just cross the gulf into Mexico," John turned the key in the ignition while stepping on the gas, "and leave all this bullshit behind." He drove toward the exit, "Want to go to the beach?" She nodded, "Okay." When John looked back the 7/11 was framed in the rearview mirror, "Would you mind," he reached over, "doing the honors," opened the glove compartment, "should be some papers in here as well," handed her the bag then shifted into third, "and close the window so it doesn't blow away." Suzanne placed her right hand on the knob and rolled up the window. The glove compartment contained a half-eaten roll of Tums, John's insurance and registration, a bootleg cassette of Hendrix at Monterey Pop, an unpaid parking ticket, a bottle opener, two spark plugs, and a pack of rolling papers. John took the can from between his thighs, "We'd have to wait until the first week in August," and sipped his beer. Subdivisions opened onto soybean fields that gave way to subdivisions—an endless looping backdrop in a warm blur of summer twilight. Suzanne crumpled a moist bud onto a paper. Three cars in the oncoming lane were followed by two more. She looked out the window as they drove by her old elementary school. The Beetle climbed Broad Bay Bridge. She sealed the joint before asking, "What about your wife?" The last thing he wanted to talk about was, "The wife," his failed marriage, "the wife wants the house, the kid, the dog," and kept his eyes on the road, "I'm just going to work one morning and never coming home." Cumulus clouds above the bay dwarfed the oil tankers lying motionless on the hazy line that divided the water and darkening sky. "The first weekend in August is next week." Faint yellow lights from fishing boats outlined stationary points in the blue distance. He took his foot off the gas, "That's why I'm," stepped on the clutch and downshifted into third, "telling you this," before they turned onto Shore Drive and sped by a seafood restaurant, another 7/11, a gas station, and a bayside hotel with its NO VACANCY sign illuminated in red neon. Suzanne's father had been killed in Vietnam when she was seven. A week after the funeral her mother left Suzanne with her parents and never came back. She received birthday cards from her mother every year postmarked from small towns in California, Texas, New Mexico and Arizona. Suzanne traced her flight by thumbing through the index of the road atlas she kept in a drawer of what was once her mother's desk, turning to the corresponding page, and pasting a silver star beside the town from where the card had been sent. Her lazy cursive on those eleven envelopes and signature scrawled beneath as many store-bought salutations were the only indications she had of a mother. The last card arrived three years ago, in the only envelope with a return address, from a small town on the Oregon coast. Her grandmother tried to convince Suzanne that the return address was a tangible invitation

And Then

and encouraged her to travel west and reconnect with her
mother. Suzanne assumed her grandparents wanted her out of
their house and was eager to comply. She moved into a dilapi-
dated beach house with her do-nothing boyfriend and five of
his stoner friends. She spent three years waiting tables while
partying with a rotating cast of surfers, dealers and aspiring
rock musicians—until the house burned to the ground. The joint
was smoking from both ends. "Why do you want me to help
you with this?" He took another hit, "I don't want help," before
handing it back, "I'm helping myself." The red taillights on the
silver Camaro disappeared beyond a bend in the road. "Why
involve me...I mean, and don't take it the wrong way, but if
this is something you can do alone." He took the joint from her,
"Where do you see yourself in five years?" "I don't know," she
sank back in the seat, "Why should you care?" He coughed into
his clenched fist, "As a Food Lion casher?" She muttered, "It's
hot in here," and rolled the window down. The smoke dissipated
as the smell of briny air filled the car. "Necessity is blind until
it becomes conscious," John turned to Suzanne, "and freedom
is the consciousness of necessity," with an expectant look, "Do
you know who said that?" Branches adorned with Spanish moss
loomed over the road. Shaking her head, "Nope." "Karl Marx
said that," he was grinning, "And do you know what it means?"
She hoped he wasn't trying to make her feel stupid, "Nope." "It
means you're already living it," John hit the joint again before
adding, "You want to go to New York," while holding the smoke
in his lungs, "So that's where you should go." A black and white
sign indicated the posted speed. Suzanne's hair was blowing in
her face, "Are you insane?" With a laugh, "Maybe I'm still a bit
crazy, but maybe," he offered her the roach, "it's the world that's
all gone wrong." "Thanks," Suzanne waved it away, "I'm really
high," and then asked, "Are you a prophet?" John chuckled while
placing the roach in the ashtray, "No, but I play one on TV," then
took his foot off the gas, "seriously though," stepped on the

clutch and downshifted into third, "What do you see yourself doing in five years?" as they made a left onto Atlantic Avenue. "I can't believe that you, or anyone, would do something like this... I mean for me, you're doing it for yourself... alright... because you are crazy... and in the best way." Rows of wooden houses faced narrow sandy streets that ended before the dunes. "It isn't my money in the first place," John downshifted into second, "why shouldn't I share it?" "Wouldn't you want me to come with you?" "Hell yes," John activated the blinker, "but I won't kidnap you," while turning off the avenue, "even if I know it's for your own damn good." They parked alongside a hurricane fence. "Where will you go?" With a nod to the air-freshener, "Big Pine," hanging from the rearview mirror, "where I should have gone in '72." She got out of the car while he changed into a pair of cut-offs and a T-shirt. Suzanne caught a glowing firefly, "You know my mother," it slowly crawled around her wrist, "did that same thing to me," before drifting away on a warm breeze. He closed the door then asked, "Did what to you?" They climbed a narrow trail through the knee-high grass. "Just left one day," the beach was nearly deserted, "after my father died." Waves pushed against the shore in sets of three. "That's probably what she thought was best for you," he turned to her and quietly added, "in my case it's the right thing to do." She looked closely at his face, "Why is that?" John noted her intent look before claiming, "He'll be much better off without me."

Sunlight reflected in the windows occasionally flashed off the chrome of the passing cars. It was June first on a fixed income. A few sparrows sang in the small puddle beneath the leaking fire hydrant. He set the crossword book down and removed his glasses. The leggy brunette in the blue mini-skirt smiled his way while returning from the park with her small black and white dog. He needed an eight-letter word for courage. Candy wrappers ringing the narrow tree trunk. He flicked the ash off

his bummed cigarette. Bravery was seven letters and spirit was
only six. The young Puerto Rican mother passed by with her
black haired boy in tow. The sweet stench of garbage fermenting
in the metal cans. The orange tomcat slipped beneath the front
wheels of a parked Toyota before crossing the street. It wasn't
even eleven and it was already too hot. The rhythmic alarm of
the delivery truck as it slowly backed up. Thunderstorms were
forecasted for the afternoon.

I asked the waitress for a chocolate donut and told her I didn't
need a bag. She handed me the donut with a serrated sheet
of wax paper folded over it, "That will be ninety cents," and
two napkins. I removed a dollar from my wallet and gave it to
her. She rang up my purchase then handed me a dime. When
I thanked her she told me to have a nice day. I pocketed the
dime, pushed open the door and ate the donut while walking to
the corner. I wiped my mouth with the napkins then dropped
them and the wax paper into a trashcan before descending the
stairs at the subway station entrance.

"Why are you doing this again," Suzanne cleared her throat
before adding, "after promising me you wouldn't?" Another cold
Sunday with intermittent rain all weekend. Brian finally roused
Suzanne out of bed and onto the phone, "It just happened," faint
light seeping through the blinds, "but I guess you've got," in
the front windows, "every reason to be pissed off," of the grey
tenement across the street. She discovered her Marlboros on
the kitchen table, "That you're fucking up again," and shuffled
across the Linoleum in a thick pair of wool socks, "Or because
you've been calling all day?" The headline atop the bundle of
newspapers piled near the curb **Sadat In Jerusalem As Israel
Bombs Lebanon** was accompanied by grainy black and white
images of a cratered city intersection and a burning hospital.
"I'm sorry but," Brian sunk his hands into the front pockets of

his jeans, "I haven't slept in five days." Steam hissed through the narrow pipe to the left of the window. She removed a cigarette from the pack, "This is exactly," put it between her lips, "this is exactly what happened," pulled a match from the book, "we had this conversation," and struck it twice on the back, "a week ago," finally lighting the cigarette, "Why are you so afraid of me?" All his doubts about her turned into a sinking feeling of betrayal. "It was more like a month ago... and don't say that because I know that you know better." She dropped the match in the glass ashtray, "You promised me that you weren't doing this anymore," sat in a chair before exhaling, "and nobody is up here with me." "I just walked here from Brooklyn," the army knapsack slung over his right shoulder contained his Nikon, "I don't want to go home," and the color photographs of her from Rockaway Beach, "so let me in."

The skinny young man with the black suitcase and bulging shopping bags paused in front of the building. Tenacity was an eight-letter word for courage. He eyed the number stenciled above the door and set the bags down. The old man on the stoop, "Who are you looking for?" resembled a run-down version of Gene Hackman. "Nobody," the address inked on his palm was still legible, "but I think I might be in the right place." His smile exposed three crooked teeth, "There aren't any nobodies living here," in an otherwise vacant mouth, "this is the most exclusive building in the neighborhood," the cigarette planted between two thick fingers was trailing smoke. The suitcase his mother insisted on packing for him had killed his right arm, "I'm staying at professor Avloniti's place for the summer," the shopping bags were filled with books, "I'm watching her cat while she's in Greece." The old man removed his cap and scratched his forehead, "Which floor?" He pulled a ring of numbered keys out of his pocket, "The fourth." "That's Paula," he examined his nails, "our resident scholar," before fixing the cap on his head,

And Then

"Did she tell you about the garbage days?" "No, but she said she was leaving me instruct—" "Monday and Wednesday for regular garbage." The young man nodded, "Okay." Taking a final drag off the cigarette, "Friday for recycling," then exhaling smoke. Another nod, "Okay." In some past life he was giving orders, "All of your cans and bottles go in that big blue one over there," now his hand trembled while pointing at the garbage cans, "Bundle up all of your newspapers." He dropped the cigarette on the step, "Because if you don't separate your trash," and crushed it beneath the heel, "I'll have to do it," of a paint splattered loafer. One final nod, "Okay." Softening his tone, "I'm Russell," while sizing him up, "What's your name?" With a cautious smile, "I'm Tom." Resting his palms on his knees, "Have you got a dollar?" Tom reached into his back pocket, "I might," and removed his wallet. "I'll pay you back this afternoon," the promise accompanied a gruff confession, "I'm short for beer." Handing over the dollar, "That's okay," left Tom with a five, "don't worry about it," which was all the money he had until his father's check finally cleared. The bill was folded in half, "Thanks," and tucked into his shirt pocket, "You need some help?" Tom collected the bags in his left hand, "I got it," and gripped the suitcase handle with his right, "but thanks," hoisting everything up the stairs. A shopping bag ripped open—Marx, Engels, Trotsky, *The Oxford History of the French Revolution*, and volume two of Gramsci's *Prison Notebooks* tumbled down the steps. "I knew that was going to happen." "I'll keep an eye on these," Russell gathered up the books, "take the rest upstairs," and stacked them in a pile, "the front door is unlocked." Tom shouldered open the door, "Thanks a lot," unlocked the inner one with the key marked 2, "I'll be back in a minute," crossed the darkened lobby then struggled up four flights of stairs.

I was washing the dishes when the phone rang. "Can you get that?" A cigarette was burning between his fingers, "It's not for me," another one smoldered in the ashtray. Poker chips, two soft packs of Marlboro 100's, wallet, magnifying glass, notepad, checkbook, beige coffee mug filled with ballpoint pens, and a worn deck of cards were crowding his end of the table. "Of course it's for you." Three chairs with split brown vinyl cushions that leaked powdery chunks of yellow foam all over the floor. "It's your birthday." "So?" December sunlight filled the broad row of casement windows in the living room. "Why would they be calling here if it wasn't for you?" Brown paper grocery bags, empty cigarette cartons, five or six months worth of the *Washington Post,* beige plastic shopping bags overflowing with the blue plastic bags the *Post* was delivered in, glossy color circulars for Christmas, Thanksgiving, Halloween, Labor Day, Back to School, July 4th piled on the floor. He tried sounding resolute, "You get it." Pizza boxes stacked atop the microwave. My hands were submerged in warm water, "I'm busy." Blackened chunks of rotten countertop surrounding the sink held puddles of suds. My sister hired a maid service to come and clean his townhouse twice a month but they quit a few years ago. My father got up, "It's a robot," and made his way into the kitchen. I turned to him while saying, "You can't know that until you pick it up." He was wearing flip flops and tube socks, jeans that were baggy at the knees and stained with urine from the crotch to the waist, an oversized grey cable-knit wool sweater pocked with cigarette burns, long wispy grey beard, an eye patch coated with dried mucus, and a Band-Aid that covered most of the large open sore near his right temple. "Someone is trying to sell me something." I saw him once and sometimes twice a month during the last few years of his life. "You shouldn't be getting those calls anymore." He cleared his throat, "They still call." I washed the dishes and did his laundry, bought groceries, vacuumed the carpet, and occasionally cleaned the bathroom. "A hundred dollars says it's not a robot." Coffee grounds, dropped food, ashes, spilled milk, strands of pasta glued to the splintered linoleum floor. He had a distinctive smokers croak that I still hear while recalling this conversation. "Are you sure?" I would open the window above the kitchen sink to get some air and frequently lingered there—especially in winter. "Absolutely." The window overlooked a well-tended lawn, clusters of bushes and trees, rows of two-story red brick townhouses constructed during the Second World War, and a park bench at the foot of a towering Sweet Gum tree. A high-rise dominated the skyline while the faint drone of traffic from 395 accompanied the view. Despite his grumbling, "We'll see about that," there was no mistaking the anticipation in his voice. He picked up the phone and said hello. I turned off the faucet then dried my hands with a paper towel. He told the caller he had and muttered thanks before hanging up. Tomato sauce was smeared on my elbow. "And?" He walked through the kitchen, "The phone company was asking about the yellow pages," returned to his chair. "What?" He picked up the cards, "They wanted to know if I got the new one," and began to shuffle them. I stood in the doorway and said, "Those assholes." He turned to me with a deflated smile, "You owe me a hundred dollars." I balled up the paper towel and tossed it in the trash. The garbage disposal was still working. Filmy water vibrated in the sink before being sucked down the drain.

Brian got up early that Saturday to do his laundry then tracked down a friend who owed him ten dollars and scored some crystal meth in the process. He met Suzanne by the token booth at the Clinton-Washington G stop, "I got two hits of acid on my way over here," she exclaimed while passing through the wooden gate, "isn't that insane," that slammed behind her. The black and white images of Suzanne he'd developed and printed as the week dragged on, "Are you serious?" now seemed feeble as they finally faced each other, "Where?" Her forearm brushed his, "Right near where we met," as he led the way toward the exit, "in Washington Square." When she passed through the gate and they embraced he knew something extraordinary was happening. Suzanne was undeniably beautiful and Brian mistook that for virtue. He spent Saturday afternoon assembling his best work and hung the black and white enlargements on the taut wire running across the living room. "How much did you pay for them?" She was wearing a low-cut black polyester top that accentuated her breasts, "Ten bucks," a short denim skirt and high cork-heeled sandals, "the guy who sold them to me said I should take it with a friend." The tall front windows were wide open and passing car stereos, trolling ice cream trucks, an argument between two women about a man who happened to be standing in front of the building, kids shouting from adjacent stoops and the ones clustered around the open hydrant down the block filled the living room as he poured over the images. Scoring acid in Washington Square confirmed another part of the city's mythology Suzanne was eager to embrace. Brian had done three hits last March and tripped alone in his apartment during a blizzard, "You really shouldn't buy acid from people you don't know," nearly four feet of snow fell from the sky while he sat in an armchair before a window overlooking Lafayette Avenue while studying his perpetually morphing reflection in glowing planes of glass, "unless you like throwing your money away on little bits of paper." She turned to him and asked, "Aren't you interested?" He'd done a bump for luck, "Acid is for hippies," just before leaving to meet her at the station, "but I'm game if you are." As they climbed the stairs Brian asked, "How was the subway?" She removed a bible tract from her purse, "Really fucking weird," presented it to him, "someone gave me this," then recalled the middle-aged preacher with the greasy comb-over sweating profusely in a purple polyester suit, "and the train took forever," who demanded Suzanne accept God's salvation as she walked onto the piss soaked downtown A/C/E platform at the furnace-like West 4th street station, "I don't

And Then

know how people can do that everyday." Brian scoffed at the black and white illustration of an opened-armed Christ standing in a supermarket isle *Jesus is everywhere and awaiting your love!* "The A Train doesn't run express on the weekends." They emerged into Brooklyn sunlight, "Thanks for coming all the way out here," and Brian noted the deep blue of her eyes. He wanted to see them saturated in Kodachrome as they lingered at the top of the stairs. A cloudless afternoon like today would be perfect. She raised her eyebrows then asked, "Which way?" He pointed and then they walked by the black Chevy Nova with the shattered windshield propped up on cinder blocks.

Hello Tom,

Thank you so much for taking care of Olive. Her dry food, always make sure she has some dry food in her bowl, is in the cabinet above the sink along with enough cans of food for the summer, if you only open a new can every other day. Please feed her a quarter of a can in the evening. Cover and refrigerate the leftovers. There are two extra bags of dry food in the hall closet by the front door. If you run out of cans please buy the same flavor and brand, otherwise she will get diarrhea. The $40 I've left you should be enough for everything. She is in the habit of eating dinner between 6 and 7 EVERY NIGHT. Also, make sure that you change her water twice a day. It can get very hot in the apartment so she needs plenty of fresh water. Olive is twelve and sometimes gets neurotic when I'm away. Please try and play with her every day, at first she will probably hide from you, so give her a few days to get used to you. She likes to play with her toy mouse, fill that with fresh catnip (in the metal tea box above the sink) once a week. I hope that your time here is productive. I trust you will not have a lot of people over. I will be in Athens for a few days and then on the island of Amorgos until the first week of August. I'll call you once I'm there.
Thanks,
Paula

Donald Breckenridge

I encountered the owner of the diner and an elderly waitress standing behind the counter. They were discussing the best place to display the sign for a new online delivery service. The owner greeted me like a long lost friend while handing me the sign, "You can order what you want on there." I recognized the logo, "I've seen this advertised on the subway," placed it on the counter and asked the waitress for a coconut donut then added that I didn't need a bag. The owner proclaimed, "You can now order that on your computer through the internet." I was taken by his enthusiasm, "That's really great," although I've never purchased anything, "I hope you get more customers that way," except their donuts. "Your donuts are really great," the food has never looked appetizing, "the best in the neighborhood." Bleached color enlargements lining the walls above the counter are backlit by dim fluorescents and feature dozens of greasy dishes made with the cheapest ingredients available. The waitress handed me the donut with a serrated sheet of wax paper folded over it, "That will be ninety cents," and two napkins. I removed the dollar from my wallet and handed it over while wondering if a purchase this small would make the minimum for free delivery. If I asked the owner that, even if he knew I was joking, it would only prolong our conversation. He proclaimed, "This will change the way my customers order food." The waitress rang up my purchase then handed me a dime. When I thanked her she told me to have a nice day. I pocketed the dime then congratulated the owner while pushing the door open.

"Is it your heart," Suzanne crossed her right leg over her left knee, "or your phone that's broken?" His hands were numb from the cold, "I was waiting for your call." The semi-transparent pink nylon curtain before the kitchen window filtered the dim grey light. "How do you wait for a phone call when your ringer is off?" Rain was dotting the windshields of the parked cars. The curtain obscured the fire escape and the tall bare oak dominating the back lot. The wind swept yellow pages torn from a phone book along the sidewalk.

Tom put the money in his wallet as a sleek black cat with gold eyes appeared in the doorway. Olive meowed a few times before crossing to the empty bowls beneath the window. He followed the cat while calling her name then unlocked the window and opened it. She leapt onto the sill and perched there, sniffing the outdoors through the screen. Merengue from a nearby radio drifted into the kitchen. He ran a tentative hand down her silken back. An elderly woman was watering the tomato plants on her fire escape. Tom hadn't lied when he said he loved cats. He worshiped Professor Avloniti—so naturally he loved her cat—if she had called him the day before leaving the country for ten weeks and asked him to baby-sit an apartment full of venomous snakes he would have readily agreed to the honor without hesitation. Professor Avloniti had beautiful brown eyes and radiated a sublime sensuality. Maybe they were living together and she was simply away for ten weeks. Perhaps they were happily married, and she was taking care of her mother who was slowly dying in Athens. His brilliant wife could be revising her memoirs at a remote writers colony, or fomenting revolution in Central America, or maybe she needed some time alone and he selflessly agreed to a long summer pause. She said she would call in a few days but would she write to him as well? The collar of his shirt was damp with sweat and his armpits clung to the sleeves. What is ten lonely weeks when you're committed to a lifetime of fidelity?

I removed the metrocard from my wallet and swiped it at the turnstile. A woman picked up her baby in the stroller and hoisted it over a turnstile. Another woman was pushing an old man in a wheelchair. They were headed toward the stairs leading to the Manhattan bound trains. A rowdy group of high school kids

Donald Breckenridge

were on the platform yelling at each other and clearly enjoying the aggravation they were causing around them. All of the seats on the bench were taken—the West Indian homecare attendant eating a bag of BBQ potato chips, two old Asian women talking quietly, a teenage boy dressed in black with techno leaking out of his earbuds and two teenage girls in Catholic school uniforms engrossed in their cell phones.

Brian wanted to photograph Suzanne in the ocean while silhouetted by the rising sun. He jumped out of bed to retrieve a book and returned flipping through pages. He found the Botticelli reproduction then passed her the book. They could go to the nudist-end of Riis Beach, if they left now they might be there by dawn. She agreed to be his Venus only if they took a cab to the beach. She also agreed to pay for the car. He took two rolls of color slide film from the refrigerator door before calling the car service. Coltrane was on the radio and they smoked in silence while listening to an endlessly cascading solo. Brian attached a wide-angle lens to his Nikon then loaded a roll of film into the camera.

Tom removed a glass from the dish rack, filled it with water and gulped it down. The framed color photograph of a naked woman standing on a beach hung on the wall to the left of the phone. Her sun-dazed expression and bright blue eyes, supple breasts, shimmering torso, faint triangle of straw colored pubic hair, long legs astride with both feet planted in the damp brown sand as a breeze drew her blonde hair away from her shoulders.

In 1968 (the same year I was born and adopted) the doctors removed a small growth from the tear duct of my father's left eye. Further tests revealed a massive brain tumor behind his nose. After being told of his condition, he overheard a group of doctors in the next room discussing his x-rays, and one doctor expressed surprise he was still alive, all of them doubted he would live more than a few years. He was 31. My father underwent eleven invasive brain surgeries over the next decade to remove those tumors. My brother and sister were born in '76 and '77. I believe having two biological children with my mother while fighting for his life gave him the strength he needed to defeat cancer. In the early '80's he took part in an experimental neutron procedure to rid his brain of the tumors. The operations of the previous decade had taken an awful toll on him and the doctors were out of options on how to approach his cancer. At the time only three patients were willing to undergo this experimental procedure, of those three, he was the only one who survived.

The black Plymouth Fury stopped outside the building and honked twice. Brian flicked his cigarette into the gutter before opening the rear door. They slid across the wide black vinyl backseat. The goateed driver with horned rimmed glasses and long black hair eyed them in the rearview mirror before stomping on the gas. The car raced up Lafayette then swung left against a yellow onto Classon. As they sped along the BQE a static-filled version of "Summer Breeze" gradually segued into a seemingly endless series of commercials.

(over)

Eat everything in the refrigerator otherwise it will go bad. When I was cleaning out the closet in the front room, where you are to sleep on the futon, I found two boxes of junk and a bag of clothes that I didn't have time to throw away. Throw them away or you can keep those records if you want. Feel free to use my desk and the typewriter but it would be best not to use my computer.

When the donut was gone I wiped off the corners of my mouth with the napkins then dropped them and the wax paper into a trashcan before descending the stairs at the subway station. I removed the metrocard from my wallet and swiped it at the turnstile. The train arrived and the doors opened. It had been a long day and I was (finally) on my way home. I took a seat. I was going uptown to my job on 207th street. I was going to the Port Authority to catch a bus. I was on my way to JFK. Our flight to Athens was in three hours. I had to catch a train at Penn Station. The Chinatown bus left for DC every other hour. I was meeting my publisher for drinks at Grand Central. My corduroy jacket was too thin and I left my scarf at the office. They couldn't start the reading without me. The subway ride to the bus that went to LaGuardia would take an hour. I had to meet with the bank manager before 5 o'clock. The library book was overdue. I promised to mail all of these documents yesterday. I needed to take a piss so hopefully the train wouldn't be delayed. I was late for my next appointment across-town and hadn't called ahead. I should have brought a book. Another warm spring evening slowly growing dark and I wouldn't get to Alexandria until early in the morning.

Brian and Suzanne met on a bench in Washington Square Park. He was engrossed in a paperback copy Genet's *Funeral Rights*. Suzanne ventured out of her room at the Hotel Earl and opted to eat a hot dog in the park, before exploring the neighborhood, and maybe shopping for clothes. Brian had bleached his hair a few weeks earlier and a safety pin hung from his left ear. Suzanne loved David Bowie and Lou Reed so she was intrigued. Dressed in the same clothes she'd been wearing since the day before, a knee- length denim skirt, black blouse and a pair of high, cork soled sandals. After wiping her mouth with a soggy napkin she finally responded to his sidelong glances by asking him what he was reading. "The story traces the paths of the peo-ple affected by, or somehow related to the death of the author's lover," Brian passed her the book, "it's like stepping through

And Then

a series of continuously unfolding mirrors." Suzanne hadn't spoken to anyone since saying goodbye to John just before midnight; aside from the beet-faced cabbie who picked her up outside the Port Authority and rattled her with horror stories about the bands of niggers and spics who were burning down Brooklyn, then dropped her off with a stern warning about the Son of Sam, and the mercifully brief conversation she had with the ghost-like desk clerk who didn't even comment on her lack of luggage after being informed that she was paying for three nights in advance with cash. Brian told Suzanne that Genet was an illegitimate child, that his mother was a maid, that she died when he was very young, that he was raised in orphanages and prisons, he was a thief and a prostitute who taught himself how to write in prison. Suzanne handed Brian the book while claiming that she had never heard of him. With a dismissive shrug Brian claimed, "He's a very important writer." She silently wondered if he was queer before asking if he cut his own hair. He nodded then asked her where she was from. "Virginia," she took a sip of Coke, "I got here this morning on a Greyhound Bus." Sunlight spilled through the motionless trees. "Cool, how long are you here for?" She leaned back on the bench, "I don't know," and declared, "but I'm never going back there." Brian had a friend living in the East Village, "Her name is Paula," a Greek girl studying history at Cooper Union, "and she's really cool," who might still be looking for a roommate, "if you're serious about staying." The man with the handlebar moustache took another handful of breadcrumbs from the brown paper sandwich bag and scattered them before a cluster of pigeons. "Are you a student?" Suzanne asked. "I'm a photographer," Brian grinned, "at least that's what it says on the overpriced piece of paper my parents bought me." Since graduating in June, "I'm moving into a loft on Mercer Street with some friends in September," Brian had been making the gallery rounds although he hadn't landed any promising connections. "Where is that?"

He studied her wide blue eyes, "In Soho," the slight smudge of mustard on her upper lip, "but for now I'm still out in Brooklyn," and the mole on her cheek to the left of her full mouth. She blinked twice, "Is that safe?" Brian hadn't had a girlfriend in two years and hadn't had sex since—with the exception of a furtive blowjob in the bathroom at Max's during a Voidoids' show last March. "Sometimes," he removed the camera from his knapsack, "Can I take your picture?" She nodded, "Hang on a sec," and wiped her mouth with a soggy napkin. He framed her face in the viewfinder then focused before pressing the shutter. A few days later Suzanne left the Hotel Earl and moved into Paula's apartment.

Three brown eggs in a blue Styrofoam carton, a navel orange, a dried up lemon, half a can of cat food covered in aluminum foil, what looked like chicken and broccoli in a Chinese takeout container. The door racks held a bottle of Rolling Rock and a jar of cherry preserves. The freezer contained a nearly empty quart of chocolate ice cream, three frost covered ice trays, a palm-sized ginger root in a clear plastic bag and a liter of imported vodka. Tom didn't like vodka and it had been three weeks since his last drink.

I would dab at the sores with a paper towel I'd soaked in rubbing alcohol before covering them with an over the counter ointment for Staph infections. "That hurts." After searching the Internet I'd concluded that the puss-filled lesions, which were black around the edges and gradually tearing through his broad forehead—already scarred by repeated brain surgeries—was a Staph infection. "Does it burn?" The most familiar looking images of Staph infections that I found on the Internet were from photographs of corpses. The sweet smell of rotting skin is stronger than cigarette smoke. He looked up at me with obvious discomfort, "It tingles." In the summer of '04, a horn-

And Then

like bump appeared on his forehead, instead of consulting a doctor and getting it removed, he simply cut it off with a pair of scissors.

Suzanne removed her sandals at the bottom of the stairs, "You never think of the ocean when you think of New York City," the sand was cool beneath her bare feet, "but this is a really nice beach." The hollow sound tall waves make as they roll against the shore. Standing naked on the beach and facing the sea—orange sunlight highlighting her blue eyes and a warm breeze moving through her shoulder-length blonde hair—with a distant full moon filling in the upper left corner of the image. Brian asked her to swim out, "Maybe fifty feet and then come back really slowly," before taking a picture of her walking into the rush of a receding wave. Three photographs as she turned toward the sun, took a few steps into the waist-high surf, and dove beneath a towering wave. He peeled off his clothes as she swam out beyond the breakers. The velvety blue sky was still studded with stars. A group of gulls gathered around their discarded clothes. Brian waded in with the camera raised above his head. Suzanne could touch her toes on the cold bottom before and after the passing swells. She was a silver silhouette amidst a warm spray of foamy blue green water. Sunlight flooding the viewfinder highlighted her torso as prisms gathered around the edge of the lens. Six months later the image of Suzanne, arms outstretched and legs suspended above a rush of pale foam, landed Brian his first group show at a gallery on 57th street and a brief mention in the *Times*.

Also, there is a bag of cat litter in the bathroom beside the sink but you'll need to buy more. Please change the box every other week. Don't dump the cat litter down the toilet because it will overflow. You'll have to bag it up and throw it out. Rinse out the cat box and let it dry before you put in fresh litter. And make sure the bathroom door is always open wide enough for Olive to get inside otherwise she'll pee on the bed!!!

Seated across from me were two teenage boys in blue tracksuits and running shoes, an Orthodox Jew with poor eyesight reading the Talmud, an old woman staring vacantly at the subway floor.

Brian took the A to West 4th then walked into Washington Square and sat wistfully on the bench where he met Suzanne before meandering up to Broadway with his hands jammed in his pockets (occasionally trying his luck with her number on a few working payphones) while gradually making his way over to her East Village walkup. "I was fucking up out in Brooklyn...And if you'd just listen to me for thirty seconds." "Do you know how stupid you sound right now?" "I'm really, really sorry." Suzanne was wearing an oversized light blue polyester shirt with the buttons undone to her navel, "You're really, really, really, really, really, really..." The recording of the operator demanding ten cents interrupted his vow, "—ver happen again." "You really, really, really shouldn't have woken me up." The black shopping bag, "It got really weird the last time we were together," adorning the tree in front of her building, "I just needed some time to figure this out," billowed in the wind. "Anyway," Suzanne interjected, "I have a date tonight," before hanging up.

Tom rinsed the bowls in the sink before filling one with cold water. Olive watched from the windowsill as he crossed the kitchen and placed the bowl of water on the floor. He wiped the other bowl off with a paper towel before filling it with dry food.

Cigarettes effectively mute your sense of smell and it's only hours after leaving a smoke filled environment that it returns. My sense of smell would come back on the bus, usually just a few miles before we pulled into the Baltimore Travel Plaza,

And Then

although I knew what to expect, the stench of nicotine on my hair and clothes always embarrassed me.

Suzanne spent days painting the apartment and getting stoned— the Puerto Rican teenagers selling loose joints near the band-shell in Tompkins Square jostled for her crisp bills—while blasting Blondie's *Plastic Letters* on the portable turntable she bought off a junkie's blanket for ten dollars. The metal gates were pulled back and the windows were wide open. It had been five weeks since she'd left home. Late afternoon sunlight covered a portion of the sagging wood floor. The apartment was filled with music, the smell of house paint mingled with marijuana and brewing coffee, as she double coated the walls and ceiling of each room. She spent most nights in clubs and bars—living in NYC with a seemingly endless supply of cash made her happier than she ever thought was humanly possible.

Russell took the beer from Tom, "You didn't have to do that," then added, "but thanks," while twisting off the cap. Tom sat beside him, "I'm supposed to eat everything in the fridge before it goes bad." "We wouldn't want that to happen," he took a swig before asking, "Are you a history major?" Tom always sounded defensive when saying, "I'm writing my thesis on the Paris Com-mune," because he'd nearly convinced himself that he would never finish it. Russell nodded, "Graduate?" "Undergrad," Tom shrugged, "the actual commune only lasted two months, and it's taken me that long to get through half of the reading list." Raising the bottle, "Well," and taking a pull of beer before say-ing, "Paula must think pretty highly of you if she is letting you stay in her place." "I've got such a crush on her," Tom confided. Russell nodded, "She's got quite a body," before adding, "but she's batting for the other team." "What do you mean?" Cough-ing into his clenched fist, "Just what I said," the words rattled around his throat, "You're the first guy who has been up there in at least ten years." Tom couldn't acknowledge the news, "I was going to spend the summer at my mom's out in College Point," and wouldn't change the subject, "How long have you known Paula for?" Russell pulled out a handkerchief, "Fifteen years or so," while rasping, "when she moved into the building," then hacked into it. The orange tomcat reappeared, "How long have you been here?" scaring the sparrows into the tree. The cat drank from the puddle. "Since sixty-five," Russell stuffed the handkerchief in his shirt pocket, "when I came back from New Mexico." Tom was disappointed, "That's pretty typical," but not surprised. This news came from the thick brush of a persistent curse. "What's that?" The more exotic and intelligent a woman, "What you just told me," the more inaccessible she had to be, "It happens to me all the time." Russell sipped his beer before asking, "You like dykes?" Tom never lacked female companionship, "All women seem out of reach," yet it was impossible for him to appreciate anyone for more than a few months, "at least the good ones." "It sounds like you enjoy making things hard for yourself." "What do you mean?" "Chasing ideals will make you miserable while a good woman will keep you grounded." A panel truck sped by tagged in blue by BK DOG, another circled A in red, an orange Batman symbol and Crack—Crack—Crack spray-painted in huge black letters on the rear doors. "And you've got both feet on the ground?" "Not when I was your age," the old man laughed, "but now I'm on all fours." "Like a turtle?" He nodded, "Exactly." "What were you doing in New Mexico?" The beer was prying off the hangover when he noticed the mailman halfway down the block—taking his sweet time. "Trying to raise a family," Russell drained the bottle, "listen kid," gripped the railing, "I've got to get out of this heat," and winced while pulling himself up. "Sure," Tom nodded, "thanks for looking after my books," while the memory of the men his mother paraded through their house in the weeks and months after his father moved out invaded the stoop. Russell descended

And Then

the stairs, "Nothing to it," made his way over to the blue can,
"I'll see you around," and dropped the bottle on the empties.
Tom watched him shuffle along the sidewalk then accost the
mailman. A police car cruised down the block.

When you sleep time no longer exists. Sleep is the best relief
for pain. Death is better but you cannot will yourself to death.
The sores gradually burrowing into his forehead began as an
ugly thumb-size wound that appeared above his right temple
in the late spring of '08. He refused to see a doctor and the
infection gradually spread from there. My father passed two
kidney stones that summer, alone and lying on a couch in his
sweltering living room, with a broken air conditioner, no fan,
and the windows closed. When I saw him that August, I begged
him to go to the hospital, pleaded with him, cursed him, and
ultimately failed to convince him to get any medical attention.
A few years earlier my siblings and I attempted an interven-
tion—to get him to give up his car, sell the townhouse and move
into an assisted care facility—we only succeeded in hurting his
feelings. "I think that means that it's working." He was tired of
living and wanted to die but dying is hard work. "How would
you know?" Understanding why someone you love wants to
die isn't the same thing as accepting that decision. "I don't."
Standing by as my father continuously refused medical care
while living in absolute squalor was one of the hardest things
I have ever experienced. "Why don't you go see a doctor?" If
you can go through your life without entering into this kind of
agony, you may be short on experience, but you are very for-
tunate. "I've had enough doctors." We were nearing the end of
our very long thread. "Then tingles means it's working." I stood
above him and applied band-aids to what became the lethal
skull infection that killed him ten months later. I was completely helpless and tremendously grateful for all of the time
we had together. My father lived far beyond everyone's expec-

tations. I was so afraid that he would die at any time, and my only regret, now that he is gone, was not lingering after saying goodbye. I never rushed out the front door but leaving him in that filthy townhouse after we embraced always made me feel unkind.

The oscillating fan atop the radiator was quietly turning over humid air. Paula was leaning on the doorframe and smoking a cigarette. She was dressed in flared jeans and a short-sleeve orange polyester shirt with a dozen silver bracelets on her left wrist. Her almond-shaped dark brown eyes and large breasts offset her somewhat masculine features. A paint splattered wooden stepladder was propped against the metal door.

The two Canadian whiskey boxes were stacked beside the black garbage bag filled with women's clothes. The top box held a pair of size 7 black patent leather sling backs with three-inch heels and an oversized black leather purse that contained three tubes of dark red lipstick, black fingernail polish, a dusty emery board, dark blue eye shadow and black eyeliner, a large orange hairbrush nested with blonde hair and an empty coin purse. The second box contained a dozen records; glam through disco-era Bowie, *The Velvet Underground and Nico* album with the banana peel removed, Lou Reed's *Transformer*, Blondie's *Plastic Letters*, T Rex's *Electric Warrior*, Television's *Marquee Moon* and Roxy Music's *Siren*. Tom still listened to hardcore, exclusively, and thought he could probably get fifteen dollars cash or a twenty-five dollar store credit for the records at Sounds on St. Marks. The manila envelope contained six black and white contact sheets and eight 8×10 black and white enlargements. He recognized the blonde from the kitchen wall in all of them. Seated on a bench in what looked like Washington Square, standing beside a parking meter, hands on her hips in front of a news-stand, standing in the middle of an empty crosswalk, looking

And Then

into the camera while holding a payphone receiver to her left ear, sitting pensively in the back of a cab, standing on the ledge of a high rise with the illuminated Empire State building in the background, lying naked on a bare mattress in the same room he was now standing in while admiring her body. The box also contained the same paperback edition of *Naked Lunch* he tried to read in high school. Tom examined the orange flyer for a Halloween event at the Paradise Garage and wondered if Paula had gone through some brief disco phase. Who was this woman, she was pretty enough to be a model, and how was she related to Paula? Were they lovers, or was she just a roommate who left her things behind? And why did Paula wait until now to have him throw all of her things away?

He would go weeks without answering the phone. I would call the fire department and ask them to check up on him and tell them to tell him to call me. I got so fed up with being unable to reach him after the third or fourth time of calling the fire department that I took a Chinatown bus down to DC and woke him up long after midnight. The ringer was off because answering the constant barrage of telemarketing calls was a pain in the ass and he forgot to turn it back on. Getting those calls to stop was as easy as putting him on a do not call list. Surviving could have been as simple as making some appointments then taking cab rides to clinics. His insurance offered fairly good coverage but getting him to care about his health was impossible. "Ok, doctor." He was still smoking three or four packs of cigarettes a day depending on how many hours he slept and only left the house to go to the supermarket. "It's almost finished." The ancient looking man with grey hair and a scraggly beard, eye patch, glasses with thick lenses and black frames, brown windbreaker, white dress shirt, worn at the knees blue jeans, canvas sneakers stained with nicotine slowly pushing a shopping cart through the Giant on South Glebe Road once a week. That was my father.

Donald Breckenridge

Maybe you saw him there? He always paid with a check. His diet consisted of waffles drowned in syrup, black coffee, tall glasses of milk, candy bars, ice cream, occasionally canned vegetables, bananas, sometimes pasta, mashed potatoes, and choice cuts of beef that would frequently begin to rot in the fridge before he got around to cooking them—unless one of us found the souring Styrofoam packages first and threw them away.

A car blasting rock music slowly passed on the street below the open windows. Suzanne stripped the sheets from the mattress, balled them up along with the pillows and dropped everything in the closet. She set the gallon of white paint, metal tray and roller on the pages of newspaper. **David Berkowitz's Letter To Jimmy Breslin From Kings County Medical Center** Paula was proud of not owning a television and the radio in the kitchen she scavenged off the street rarely worked. The portable turntable transformed their apartment. Paula checked out a dozen Maria Callas records a few days before Callas died of a heart attack in Paris. Although Suzanne found opera incredibly boring she engaged Paula in her enthusiastic descriptions of their plots and intrigues. **Beame Takes Heat From Koch** When asked why she hadn't bought a turntable if the music she loved could be checked out from the library, Paula shrugged before claiming that it hadn't been a priority, then thoughtfully added that living in New York made it too easy to forget about all of the real things that give you pleasure. **Jet Engine Blows-Rains Metal on LI** On those rare nights when Suzanne stayed home, arias would slip through the crack beneath the door as she drifted off (over-caffeinated and baked) then harmonize with the random sounds from the street. **Hurricane Anita Moving in on Galveston TX** Paula moved to New York in the summer of '75 to attend Cooper Union. She was majoring in European history with an emphasis on the emergence and struggles of the French Labor Movement. Her older brother,

And Then

Fedro, had been killed on the final day of the Athens Polytechnic uprising when the army, under orders from the military junta, massacred the students occupying the campus. Suzanne slid the can of paint closer to the wall by tugging on the pages of newspaper. The black and white image of president Carter at a news conference accompanied the quote, *There is no doubt the energy shortage is here and it's going to approach the crisis stage in the near future.* The day after his murder the family fled to England where they were granted asylum. Paula's father, a widely published Marxist academic, began teaching at the East London Polytechnic. The autobiographical account of his arrest, torture and imprisonment that began in April of '67, when the military took over Greece, *Years in the Shadows,* was translated into seven languages. Suzanne crossed the room to retrieve the tray and roller. Her mother remained despondent over the death of her son, and felt that Paula had abandoned the family by opting to live in New York. Suzanne poured a dollop of paint into the metal tray. The monthly stipend Paula received from her family covered her expenses while Suzanne unknowingly paid the entire rent on the 4th floor walkup. Paula had very few friends and only left the apartment to attend classes, buy books or check them out from the library. She read two or three novels a week and was fluent in four languages. Paula spent most of August reading, *A la recherché du temps perdu,* while lying naked in her narrow bed beneath a whirling box fan. She supplemented her income by occasionally translating for an academic press, and tutoring the children of wealthy Greek merchants. Paula believed most men were part of a dull, needy species, while a select few belonged to a vengeful tribe of dangerously competent monsters. Suzanne slowly moved the roller over a large ash-colored handprint and what might have been dried streaks of blood. Paula recalled finding a syringe wedged between the floorboards—toxic detritus from her old roommate who vanished one hot July night with his guitar and bedroll—as she watched the widening patch of white paint cover the wall. Paula's fleeting encounters with pretty, bi college girls rarely lasted more than a few weeks. The losing streak of superficial American girls who lacked her emotional depth and intellectual curiosity had left her reeling.

All of Paula's Love Letters

The bottom drawer of the metal beige filing cabinet beside Paula's desk contained the letters from Ursula, Françoise and Anna. They were bundled by sender, bound with lavender ribbons and arranged in chronological order. The letters were enclosed in the envelopes they had been mailed in but all of the stamps had been removed. The oldest bundle—January '76 through July of '79—contained Ursula's letters to Paula. Although Ursula was German her English was concise, yet awkward in the more detailed passages, and her handwriting (always in black ink from a fountain pen that covered both sides of nearly transparent paper) was only laboriously legible. The letters from Anna—May '81 through September '86—were written entirely in Greek. While the letters from Françoise—June '85 through November '88—were sweetly scented and scrawled in nearly illegible French. Tom's passable Spanish was useless. He couldn't decipher much more than the names of authors quoted (Sappho, Beckett, Proust, Musil, Bachmann, Wolf, Rilke, Brecht, Rich, Celan, Jelinek, Camus, Char) travel dates and destinations—London, West Berlin, Munich, Amsterdam, Barcelona, Rome, Vienna, Paris, Lyon, Milan, and Athens. Anna's pages contained sketches from terraced vineyards near the Brenner Pass in Sud Tyrol, impressions of a village square somewhere in Savoy beneath Mont Bisanne, drawings of the haunted caves in Eboli, and sketches of the small fishing ports found on the islands dotting the Aegean Sea. With the help of a Greek dictionary, Tom learned that S'agapo means I love you. Françoise occasionally included advertisements for a chocolate bar (torn from the color pages of glossy magazines) that featured a pair of cartoon foxes dressed in pleated skirts, white blouses and bonnets in her multicolored, indecipherable missives. When signing off, Françoise nearly always scrawled J'taime, but sometimes, in the letters she sent Paula just before and after they had seen each other, she would write J'adore. One night, Tom stayed up until dawn and read the nearly two hundred letters from Ursula. She was ten years older than Paula, who at the time was in her early twenties and still a student at Cooper Union. Ursula was interested in corresponding with Paula after meeting her father at a party celebrating the West German publication of *Years in the Shadows*. Their relationship became physical when Ursula visited New York for the first time in the fall of '77. Her letters portrayed a frustrated leftist growing disillusioned with her existence as a result of the incredibly oppressive political situation in West Germany. Throughout the '70s the Office for the Protection of the Constitution (Amt für Verfassungsschutz) employed many of the same tactics the Nazi's utilized to suppress and control the population. In '75 alone they screened nearly a half-million civil service applicants and any academic, doctor, social worker, librarian, etc, applying for a government position who was currently or once belonged to a leftist organization, participated in leftist demonstrations, or even subscribed to journals the government deemed leftist were rejected for civil service vacancies regardless of how qualified they might have been for the position they were applying for. Husbands were denied employment because of their wives' involvement in leftist organizations, commune members were rejected for positions because of what other members might have done, even family members were held responsible for the activities of each other. Ursula had been a member of the SDS and was arrested during a demonstration in the summer of '68. In the fall of '72 she was detained after a police raid on a suspected RAF safe house in West Berlin. Although neither incident led to a single conviction (or even a fine) they were used against her when she applied for a research position that was to examine the nefarious roles multinational corporations played in the coup that had taken place in Greece, and how those corporations profited from the nascent police state. She was falsely accused of belonging to the outlawed Communist party, and although nothing was actually done to prove her membership, that accusation was enough to block her application and it earned her a career ban. A year later when the university selected Ursula for a teaching position the Office for the Protection of the Constitution forced the university to reject her. Her family, friends and lovers would not visit her at home because they could not afford to be identified with her politics. The rest of the text was genuinely passionate, occasionally even graphic, and contained detailed recollections of their lovemaking. Tom masturbated to their color Polaroids. It soon became apparent that Ursula was Paula's first love. They shared a deep emotional connection, and in the spring of '78 Ursula traveled to London to be with Paula when she came out to her parents. In spite of Ursula's proclamations, devotion and determined long distance fidelity, the letters left Tom feeling empty. Those words were written a decade ago, and never intended for anyone other than Paula, certainly not Tom, and inevitably, after his arousal wore thin, reading them became tiresome. Their affair came to a terse stop in July of '79. Two weeks after what must have been a very difficult, final trip to Rome, Ursula broke off contact in a brief letter (mailed from a boarding school in Basel where she finally found work) that curtly acknowledged their growing differences and ended with, *This distance has been tearing against us since the very beginning and I don't have the will or energy to make it work anymore.* When Tom turned off the desk lamp a grainy dawn filled the room. Olive watched from the windowsill as he lay down on the futon and closed his eyes. He fell asleep almost immediately.

And Then

What Tom Discovered in the Park

Three Messerschmitts suspended from his bedroom ceiling were closing in on a disabled B-17. Black smoke billowed from all four engines. Machine gun fire ripped through the fuselage as the Messerschmitts roared past the shattered cockpit. Tom tried to radio the crew and discovered that the control board was on fire. His co-pilot bled to death as the Messerschmitts circled back for a final pass. Tom clambered through the doomed plane as bullets ricocheted around his head. The side gunners were slumped in a large pool of frozen blood. The rear of the plane was engulfed in flames. Tom forced open the escape hatch. A blurred black and white winter landscape appeared far below. Giant clouds of flack pocked the sky. He cocked and holstered his .45 before leaping toward the earth.

Tom's father stepped on the gas while asking, "Do you get along with him?" The beige sedan accelerated through the intersection. His stomach began throbbing after lunch—half a tuna sandwich, two bites of a sour pickle, a few potato chips—and a metallic film coated his mouth. Hot air was blowing out of the vents as Dionne Warwicke sang, "Don't Make Me Over" on the a.m. radio. The diner was in Woodside, "Yeah," around the corner from his father's new apartment, "I guess so." A brand new convertible sofa and the green recliner from the living room were now situated before the portable black and white bedroom television. The refrigerator contained a six-pack of beer, a quart of milk, a loaf of bread, a dozen eggs, a jar of strawberry jam, jars of mustard, horseradish and mayonnaise, a pound of bacon, cold cuts wrapped in wax paper, three rock-hard tomatoes packed in cellophane, and a wilted head of lettuce. The previous tenant left behind a wood-grained Formica table and four brown chairs that were crowding the kitchenette. The waitress with the high, rust-colored beehive and flakey orange lipstick had pressed a Snickers bar into his palm for the ride home. The worst part about their separation was saying goodbye to his father every-other Sunday afternoon. Removing a cigarette from the pack in his jacket pocket, "I will always love your mother," he lit it with a chrome Zippo, "because without her we would have never had you," snapped the lighter shut, "You know those models that you love so much," looking at his son, "how they always come with instructions?" Tom nodded, "Yeah," a familiar headache was coming on. "And how if you follow the instructions your boat ends up looking almost as good as what is on the box." Tom palmed his forehead, "But it never looks as good as that." A large yellow banana painted on the side of a delivery truck slid past them. "They sell more of everything that way," father informed son, "by making the package look better than the product." Tom watched the banana move through the traffic. "Isn't that like a lie?" His father had both hands on the wheel, "It isn't like a lie," with the cigarette wedged, "it is a lie," between the index and middle finger of his right hand, "but it's a harmless one," grey smoke spiraled overhead. "Your mother and I," he looked in the rearview mirror before asking, "How do you get everything to work out the way that you want it to without any instructions?"

Mickey's gloved hands indicated that it was seven. Tom pulled back the covers and swung his legs out of bed. Small green soldiers surrounded the cars lined up on the pale blue carpet. The desk was cluttered with a partially constructed model of the Bismarck. The propellers and rudder were glued to the gray hull. The main guns, turrets, boats, life rafts, reconnaissance planes, cranes, masts, and range finders were molded to thin stems of gray plastic. The instructions lay beside the illustrated box that depicted the legendary battleship at sea and under heavy fire. His toy .45 was beside a stack of textbooks. Tom stepped into his Batman slippers and went downstairs for a bowl of Frosted Flakes.

And Then

The banana on the rear of the delivery truck was attached to a large rotary phone. "But you and mom got a marriage license." A Bronx address in looping red letters preceded a ten-digit telephone number. "A license and a set of instructions are two different things." His parents had been married for eleven years, "How come?" and separated for four months. They met at Queens College where his father was majoring in business and his mother in English. "A license only gives you the right to do something, like drive a car." Tom nodded. "You take a test first, and when you pass, they give you a license, then you can legally drive." His parents were both twenty-four when they married in the summer of '67. "But you don't need to take a test to get married?" Slowing to a stop in the line before the light. "Have you ever tried to build a model without instructions?" Tom was born in September of '68. "No." The traffic light swayed in the wind above the intersection. He grew up on a quiet block in College Point, down the street from Flushing Bay, in the house where his mother still lived. His father was the personnel manager of a staple factory in Long Island City. His mother taught English at an elementary school in the Bronx, just over the Whitestone Bridge. "A lot of inventors fly their own planes," his father stubbed the cigarette out in the ashtray, "you'll be so rich you might even own two of them," the light turned green, "just remember that with whatever you decide to do," the cars began to move, "always do the best job that you can," he pressed his foot on the gas, "don't do it for anyone else," and the beige sedan slowly accelerated through the intersection, "always do it for yourself."

Tom gulped down the sweetened milk. Sunlight hung on the lace curtain above the kitchen sink. The frost on the window had begun to melt. Tom heard the sound of car tires spinning on a patch of ice. He rinsed the bowl in the sink and licked the cold sweet spoon before placing it in the dishwasher.

Donald Breckenridge

His father activated the blinker and glanced over his shoulder before changing lanes. Tom eyed the black Corvette as it raced past them. A travel advisory on the radio warned listeners of a heavy snowstorm that would begin around 7 pm and taper off late the next morning. Temperatures would remain well below freezing until Thursday. Tom watched the profiles of people in the passing cars while hoping that school would be cancelled again. He slid his left hand into his coat pocket and gave the Snickers bar a reassuring squeeze.

The cat chased the mouse around the house so fast that they started a tornado that destroyed all of the furniture in the living room. The mouse ran into the kitchen with the cat snipping at his heels with a pair of garden shears. The mouse jumped onto the stove and brained the cat with a frying pan. Two sunny-side-up eggs resembling eyes and a strip of bacon for a frown ran down the cat's face. Tweeting blue birds and pulsating yellow stars circled the cat's head. Tom pressed the power button and watched the color screen quickly shrink to the size of a bright dime.

"Sometimes it sounds like he is hurting her." His father drove onto the service road, "What do you mean?" and pulled into an empty space. "Like she's crying really loud." He shifted the car into park, "It's probably just the TV," and twisted the key from the ignition, "I'll be right back." Tom watched his father step around the waist-high piles of black garbage bags and disappear behind the bar door.

Tom got dressed while standing in front of his unmade bed. He put on freshly laundered underwear, long johns, tube socks with Steelers stripes, weekend jeans and a snug green wool sweater. He sat on the edge of the bed and squeezed his feet into a new pair of winter boots.

And Then

Another Sunday in the passenger seat—mounds of blackened snow between the parked cars in waning winter light—people bundled up against the cold pushing grocery carts.

Tom quietly knocked, "Hey mom," before opening the door. The darkened room smelled faintly of her perfume. His mother and Allen were asleep. "I'm going out to play." He backed out of her bedroom and closed the door.

His father returned a few minutes later and offered him a stick of gum. He unwrapped the silver foil, "How do crazy people go through the forest?" Slowly exhaling through his nose, "Is this another one of Allen's jokes?" Stuffing the cinnamon gum in his mouth, "Yeah." Inserting the key in the ignition, "I don't know, how?" "They take the psychopath." Revving the engine, "That wasn't too bad," before shifting the car into drive.

Tom jumped off the top of the slide and tumbled through the snow. The ground shook as the B-17 exploded on impact in a nearby field. He unhooked the parachute and buried it beside a tree before running behind a nearby park bench. Making contact with the resistance while staying one step ahead of the Gestapo was going to be impossible. He fingered the cyanide capsule while contemplating his slim chances for survival. Tom spied a couple entering the park with a German Shepard on a long leash and removed the .45 from his coat pocket.

The car slowed as it approached the house. "We didn't raise you to be a sneaky kid." Tom kept his eyes on the faint grass stains on the knees of his jeans. "And I know how hard this is for you, believe me, because it's been really hard on me as well. But I don't want you to keep things from me." The car came to a slow stop. "That doesn't mean that I want you to tell me everything your mother does." His father shifted it into park.

"But why did you think it was okay to lie to me?" "Because I was afraid that you wouldn't, you wouldn't want to move back home." His father sighed, "I really don't think that is going to happen." Tom pressed his eyes closed before asking, "Why not?" "How would you like to go to the zoo the next time you spend the weekend with me?"

A Messerschmitt flew in low over the park. Tom dove into a snowdrift as it roared overhead. He watched the plane disappear into the heavy fog hanging over the bay before running toward the shore. The frozen embankment was imbedded with bleached beer cans and soda bottles, a sneaker half-frozen in the muck, cigarette butts, a large truck tire, and shotgun shell casings. A partially submerged body lay facedown in the brackish water. It looked like a mannequin, dressed in black with a blonde wig, and he stumbled over a log while walking toward it.

*

The helicopter taking Lieutenant Johnson back to Phu Bai was hit by heavy ground fire and forced down near the mouth of a river. Both pilots were seriously injured in the rough landing and the ARVN liaison officer accompanying Lieutenant Johnson had been shot in the thigh. The wingman hovered as close to the ground as possible while Lieutenant Johnson pulled the wounded men away from the smoking wreck and helped them into the helicopter. Sustained bursts of automatic gunfire opened up from behind a cluster of trees on the opposing shore. Bullets were snapping through the air as Lieutenant Johnson ordered the wingman to take off with the wounded—insisting that he could fend for himself. The downed helicopter was on fire. The Lieutenant dove into the river and was pulled along by the powerful outgoing current. He swam beneath the surface of

And Then

the warm murky water, only coming up for air when he needed it. He was hoping to make it into a calm eddy so he could drag himself back to land.

When the box fan in the kitchen window was set to medium it nearly muted the continuous flow of Merengue drifting through the apartment. Tom spread his books and notes out on the table after breakfast, which usually consisted of coffee, two boiled eggs, a glass of orange juice and a few slices of whole-wheat toast. Olive would brush by his ankles once or twice with a quiet meow then find a cool spot on the linoleum and sprawl out for a long nap. The mornings vanished when chased by a few more cups of coffee.

The West Indian nanny offering grapes to the unhappy pale child strapped in a stroller, the young Mexican mother with her two daughters wearing identical pink dresses and haircuts although one was a few years older and taller than the other, the West Africans standing around the metal pole having an animated conversation in French, a scowling Haitian teenager texting someone, the Dominican boy playing with a Spider-man action figure, an attractive brunette reading a paperback and showing plenty of thigh, two young black boys jumping on their seats antagonizing their distracted and clearly exhausted mother, an old drunk with his eyes closed and head resting on the window.

The current finally let him go and the Lieutenant found himself a few hundreds yards away from the shore. A large cluster of poles loomed even further in the distance and he began a steady crawl in that direction. The sun was setting well beyond the mouth of the river when he reached the fishing weir. The shell-encrusted pole he grabbed onto ripped his hands open but he looped an arm over a thick rope and hung on. After

Donald Breckenridge

Lieutenant Johnson caught his breath he tried to get his bearings—with two rounds left in his .45 and a full clip in his flack vest—examining the blood flowing from the deep cuts on his palms left him stunned as the terror of the crash and being shot at collided with the realization that the soldiers trying to kill him had nearly succeeded.

The apartment was never completely silent but nothing distracted Tom while sitting at the blue-green Formica table surrounded by those pink walls. He read and outlined as the circular Fluorescent light buzzed faintly overhead.

The Chinese man walked slowly through the subway car while playing something that sounded vaguely like Mozart on a bamboo flute and there was a lull in the noise as everyone took in his waltz-like refrain.

Lieutenant Johnson and the ARVN officer had been flown into a remote hamlet twenty miles south east of Phu Bai in order to deliver a solatium payment to a farmer whose wife and daughter were killed a month earlier in a friendly fire incident. The framed black and white Polaroid of the farmer's young wife cradling their baby was the centerpiece of his modest shrine. After expressing their condolences the officers got his signature on a few forms then presented him with fifty dollars worth of piasters and a carton of cigarettes. The hamlet chief oversaw the exchange as dozens of villagers silently gathered outside. Afterwards the hamlet chief related detailed information about increased VC activity in the area before the helicopters arrived to take the officers back to Phu Bai. They were flying just above the treetops as Lieutenant Johnson tried to articulate what offering such a paltry compensation felt like— telling the men he had a beautiful daughter and that he really missed his wife—when heavy ground fire raked the engine. The

And Then

pilots struggled to keep the helicopter from going down in the river or spinning into the trees just before they slammed onto the shore.

Tom felt such a remarkable sense of belonging in Paula's apartment. The tall shelves in nearly every room were over-crowded with rows of books—and piles of books on top of each row—although the furnishings were minimal all of the chairs were comfortable for reading in. A framed movie poster of Monica Vitti in Antonioni's *Red Desert* hung in the hall by the entrance and a Klee reproduction was above her bed.

The neutron procedure worked and my father beat cancer although he lost an eye and his ability to smell. His marriage ended soon after, my mother stood by him through some of the most difficult years of his life, but now found him changed physically and mentally to the point where she could no longer live with him. My parents split-up in the fall of '83 and my father moved from Virginia Beach to Alexandria. I joined him in his townhouse in the summer of '85, attended my junior and senior years of high school then lingered under his roof for another year before moving to New York City. My father never remarried, never dated, after being downsized in the early '90s he never held another job, and rarely left his townhouse with the exception of those weekly trips to the supermarket.

At night the sea was considerably warmer than the air and the sky was filled with stars. A fishing boat slid out of the darkness. Lieutenant Johnson could duck down and avoid being seen but what would happen to him once they left? He knew enough Vietnamese to yell, "Toy la ban!" *I am your friend.* The last thing he saw was the muzzle flash as bullets struck him in the head and chest.

Donald Breckenridge

Sprinklers flung streams of cold well water onto chemically treated lawns. Suzanne was walking through her deserted Sunday morning neighborhood for the last time when John pulled up in his Beetle. They smoked a bowl along the long way to their final day as wage slaves. The cash being handed to Suzanne in exchange for brown bags of groceries was to be divvied up into fat, life changing stacks. Four thousand dollars tucked into her oversized black leather purse. The assistant manager with the unhappy family and faltering mortgage hadn't deposited the cash from Friday or Saturday—his bags were packed.

Tom discovered a comfortable pair of black lace panties in Paula's underwear drawer, wearing them in her bedroom while imagining how they must look and feel on her shapely ass was a brand new thrill. Five days ago an aggressive sales pitch for a new long distance service provider preceded Paula's echoed call from Amorgos by fifteen minutes. Paula asked about Olive and expressed relief when she was informed that her cat was sleeping with Tom on the futon every night. He was following her instructions to the letter and so far everything was fine. No, he never had a cat growing up, his mother was allergic, to dogs as well, but maybe she just didn't like animals. Olive would trail him from room to room and sometimes sit on his lap when he worked. He didn't tell Paula he'd searched all of her closets, cabinets and drawers. Or confess to reading every letter he could from her former lovers. Or say anything about fetishizing her wardrobe. Or mention his experiments with her vibrator. Or relate his profound disappointment after discovering that the entire shelf of black and white Mead Composition notebooks that she used as journals for nearly a decade were written entirely in Greek. He claimed that his time in her apartment was going to be incredibly productive. She said that was what she had hoped would happen. He was extremely grateful for this opportunity. She said she was looking forward to reading his thesis in the fall. Was there a number she could be reached at in the event of an emergency? She said that would be impossible, the house didn't have a phone, the place was beautiful and it overlooked a small beach, it was just like living in a postcard, yet it was as remote as it was beautiful. Tom marveled at her description before saying that he really wanted to go to Europe sometime as well... like maybe Spain or Southern France... then silently hoped his remark didn't sound too much like an invitation. She said she was calling from the post office in the Hora, a forty-five minute bus ride away from where she was staying, then asked if there had been rioting in the park. He said no, it had been quiet, well, not really quiet, the neighborhood was rocking every night till really late, but he'd gotten used to the noise and was sleeping with the windows open. She said she was happy to be far away from New York this summer. When she thanked him again for taking such good care of Olive he pressed the receiver to his ear and reveled in the impossibly warm sound of her voice. There was a brief pause before she said she had to go, the call was really expensive, but she would definitely call again in July. Their goodbyes overlapped. Tom listened to the series of clicks accompanying the dial tone then realized he'd forgotten to ask about the woman in those photographs she wanted him to throw away.

I grabbed a few pairs of socks and some underwear. Monday was our laundry day so my options were limited. A few clean T-shirts, a dress shirt, a pair of jeans, toothbrush, the phone charger and a paperback copy of Théophile Gautier's *My Fantoms* got tossed into the backpack—although I doubted I'd be able to read on the train.

The wooden phone booth was beside the women's bathroom door. Five middle-aged men were watching the Mets lose to the Cubs on the silent color television. The bartender changed two dollars into eight quarters. Frank Sinatra was crooning about the summer wind on the jukebox. Suzanne ordered a rum and coke then removed a cigarette from the pack in her purse. The man seated on her left offered her a light. He appeared to be in his mid-sixties with bright blue eyes, close-cropped grey hair and a pale, paper-like complexion. She thanked him, exhaling smoke, as the chrome Zippo snapped shut. She placed the thin red straw in the empty black plastic ashtray. The drink was tall, strong and gone in three swallows. The dark red vinyl stools surrounding the bar had low backs and seats that swiveled. She ordered another, with less ice and more rum please, then tried to read her expression—was it bewildered or determined—reflected between the bottles of cognac—perhaps both—as the bartender mixed the drink in a fresh glass. Suzanne decided that the man beside her, who asked if she was on a mission, resembled a blue-eyed, alcoholic version of Dick Tracy. Suzanne turned to him and said she had a difficult call to make. Thanking the bartender as he placed the drink on the coaster. The calendar on the side of the cash register featured a color photograph of the Grand Canyon at sunset. There were three pale pink paper roses in the clear glass vase on the counter beneath the calendar. The picture of a grinning Billy Carter clutching a frothy pint of beer had been cut out of the *Daily News* and taped to the mirror. A small Irish flag was sticking out of the blue plastic cup filled with ballpoint pens and a few sharpened pencils. The golden yellow neon Miller High-Life sign was buzzing faintly above the cash register. Smoke from her cigarette bled into the grey cloud hanging above the bar. Suzanne tasted the lime wedge while sipping her drink. She surprised her grandparents with her well-laid plans the night before leaving and claimed she was going to travel west with all the money she earned as a cashier and track down her mother. Working full-time for minimum wage ($2.22/hr) while not paying rent for two months enabled her to save five hundred dollars. She would stop along the way and wait tables when making money became necessary. She promised to update them with postcards and phone calls, and yes, reassuring her grandmother, she'd given notice at the supermarket.

Tom hadn't touched the phone since speaking to Paula. It hung silently on the wall beside the photograph of the naked blonde. He turned off the ringer and muted the answering machine. There was no reason to pick up the phone or listen to the machine because nobody he knew had the number. He could have reached out to friends living nearby, or gone around the corner to Tompkins Square Park, or wandered the neighborhood and run into more than a few people he knew but since landing this living arrangement all social obligations felt like unnecessary distractions. He left the apartment to buy groceries on Sunday morning, three days ago, and chatting up the pretty Dominican cashier was the last conversation he had. The only people who knew of his whereabouts aside from Paula were his mother and father; she was vacationing in Barbados and he was now living in Chicago with his second wife.

Born and raised on a dairy farm in Oneida County, New York, my father was the third of six children. Photos from his teens reveal a very handsome and ambitious young man. He was the high school senior class president and the only one in his family to finish college. He earned a master's degree in mechanical engineering from the US Naval Postgraduate School in Monterey, California. He commanded a Swift Boat in Danang, Vietnam in '69 -'70 and saw combat although he never talked about it. He was the cool sailor in dress whites and the decorated officer with a storied and distinguished career. He was a plainspoken dairy farmer. He possessed an intrinsic sense of decency and extraordinary tenacity in the face of impossible odds. He was an epic procrastinator. He had a terrific sense of humor. He never locked the front door to his townhouse. He was incredibly stubborn—pigheaded to the point of being a public menace. It was only after plowing into a Metrobus and totaling his car while driving legally blind on an expired license before he started taking a cab to the supermarket. My father wasn't vain yet the drastic alterations to his physical appearance were extremely difficult for him to accept. Every look in the mirror—regardless of how diminished his sight or filthy the reflection—was a reminder of what cancer had taken from him.

Sleeping beneath packing blankets flecked with vomit and splotched with dried blood. She met Yvonne and Nick at a gay disco on King Street. Curly blond locks pooled on a pink bath towel. They befriended a bemused Suzanne after the bearded Canadian disc jockey that had dragged her there from Phoebe's disappeared around midnight with a petite Puerto Rican transvestite. Streaks of rainwater ran down the tall windows overlooking Central Park. Yvonne was a diplomat's daughter and a self-professed Anarchist obsessed with Louise Brooks. Gold parquet floors, a high molded ceiling and a gaping marble fireplace. Nick was a skinny orange haired punk with a budding heroin addiction. The ornate gilded mirror above the marble mantel reproduced a portion of the empty bookshelves spanning the length of the opposite wall. Yvonne had been tasked with overseeing the packing and closing up of this palatial apartment before joining her parents in Paris. Black stilettos, a pair of red patent leather knee-high boots, black nylons, blue cotton panties, a white dress shirt and a mini-skirt were strewn across the dusty floor. Nick lied about dropping out of Brooklyn College and told everyone who would listen that he was starting his own record label. The water in the chipped wine glass was beaded with oxygen. Yvonne was bound for the Sorbonne and guaranteed confinement in a stratum that she would continue to rebel against while living a life of privilege. A black lace bra, bamboo chopsticks and grease splotched takeout containers,

And Then

chunks of blackened aluminum foil. Yvonne and Nick's frequently hilarious Boris and Natasha meet a debased Romeo and Juliet routine finally wore thin when Yvonne vomited into Suzanne's lap after shooting a speedball. The overflowing Pan Am ashtray, a small green disposable lighter, a trail of cotton balls, crumpled bloody tissues and empty glassine bindles cluttered the top of the cardboard wardrobe box before the daybed. Suzanne removed her soiled dress in the bathroom and soaked it in the sink. After snorting and freebasing cocaine for three nights and two days with Nick and Yvonne plus an assortment of her best friends—all supposedly crushed that such an incredibly cool connection was abandoning them for Paris—Suzanne decided to try heroin. Nick dutifully cooked up a tiny bit from his dwindling stash as she tied off her left arm with a bra strap, "Make a fist," after a few near misses he hooked the thin green vein, "now let it go," with a stainless steel surgical syringe.

A loud roll of thunder got Tom up from the table and over to the kitchen window. The oak branches were shaking in the wind. He removed the fan and placed it on the floor. The rear row of buildings and towering tree obscured his view. He walked through the darkened apartment and recalled a cloudless, nearly cerulean, blue sky when waking a few hours ago. The front room smelled like rain on hot concrete. A cool wind was flipping through the pages of Sade's *Juliette* that he'd left on the futon. Menacing black clouds were piled on top of each other. He watched their ragged ends block out the noonday sun. The light above the deserted block turned from the sepia of old photographs into ominous night. In an open window across the street agile brown arms gathered up a billowing white curtain then pulled the window closed. A blonde walked quickly up the stoop and into the building. He heard the front doors slam then hurried footfalls echoed off the stairs. A flash of lightning followed by a nearly instantaneous crash of thunder created a chorus of car alarms. When the downpour began in earnest a few pale faces appeared in the windows across the street. Steam rose from the sidewalk as water overran the gutters. Tom noticed that the screens were getting soaked and closed the windows. He met a terrified Olive in the hall just before another flash of lighting and boom of thunder sent her tearing into the bedroom where she vanished beneath Paula's bed. Handwritten pages of the Marx outline were strewn across the kitchen table. The box fan blew over, crashed into the cat bowls and began knocking rhythmically against the floor. He yanked the plug from the socket, closed the window and moved the fan away from the puddle. And that was when the oblique shape drifted along the wall. Later he would claim that it was like watching the shadow of a hawk slowly glide over an open meadow. He turned around and a warm, human dampness clung to his chest and arms. The checkered Linoleum floor creaked beneath an invisible weight. The shadow gradually moved along the cabinets before slipping down the hall. Tom's heart was thumping in his throat. The kitchen was as empty as it had been all week, and yet the air was charged with energy. He took the knife from the sink and peered into the hall. The rain on the roof and occasional rumble of thunder accompanied Tom as he cautiously crept through each room with the knife clenched in his right fist. When confronting his pale, wide-eyed reflection in the bathroom mirror he noticed the butter smeared on the blade.

I called after purchasing the ticket—thinking he would be able to get off the couch, walk across the living room and answer the phone. Or maybe the phone was on the coffee table and he would be able to reach it. I wanted to tell him that I was on my way. I would be there as soon as possible. It rang and rang as I crossed Penn Station then the line went dead. I tried again and

And Then

finally gave up after a recording informed me that the person I was calling was unavailable, that I should try later. The TGIF was nearly empty. I ordered and downed a shot of Jameson's but didn't have time for another because the train to Washington was boarding.

Was the lingering smell of vomit making her nauseous? The warmth in her arm passed into her fingertips before flooding her brain then kicking her in the stomach. Suzanne had lucked into an exclusive party with some totally cool and really beautiful rich kids in a giant vacant apartment overlooking Central Park. Her weekend of jaw grinding unblinking confidence had just been run over by a crosstown bus. The mosquito-sized bite of white heroin was chasing stubborn chunks of bile around the back of her throat. Standing naked on the black and white tiles. Now they were totally out of everything. The fluorescent reflection in the wall-sized bathroom mirror gave her butterflies. Nick was yelling at Yvonne for slicing open all of the straws and licking them clean—like some fucking fiend. Suzanne just needed another minute alone to relax, maybe take a warm bath, maybe catnap for an hour or two then she could think about going home. Yvonne wasn't jealous—she was pounding on the bathroom door—as Nick pocketed the remaining bills in Suzanne's wallet. Yvonne just knew that Nick wanted to fuck Suzanne—no I'm not going to shut up, why don't you shut up, you're not even going to miss me. Her legs finally gave out and she crumpled on the tiles. Nick called Yvonne a freak and made sure to slam the front door. Yvonne's narrow alabaster face, "What are you doing on the floor?" pocked with acne and framed by a blue-black bob. Nobody was around Sherman Square that early on a Monday morning in the pouring rain. Suzanne coughed up a mouthful of whatever was making her gag before rasping, "I was going to take a bath," then wiped her hands on a wad of toilet paper. Nick had to take the 2 Train up to 125 and Lenox to score.

"That was quite a storm." The sky was clearing although a few people were walking around with open umbrellas. "It should cool things off a bit," Russell was wearing the same clothes when they met six weeks ago, "How's it going up there?" He was sitting on a week-old copy of the *Post*. Tom forced a grin, "Okay, I guess." A leafy branch had been tossed on the sidewalk. The clouds reflected in the puddles were fleeing patches of blue sky. Russell dropped the cigarette on the step and crushed it beneath the heel of a paint-splattered loafer. "You've been cooped up there the entire time?" A cab came to a stop in front of the building. Tom nodded, "I think maybe I need some air." A young Japanese woman in a shimmering blue mini-dress and black patent leather heels got out of the cab. "Meanwhile," Russell placed his hands on his knees, "the big beautiful world out here," and leaned forward, "is just passing you by." The cab drove off and they watched the woman step over the tree branch. Tom wasn't prepared to describe what he saw in the kitchen, "I guess so," it wasn't just in his head, "I might go and grab a bite to eat," but if anyone would know about the roving shadows that inhabited the building, "like some Sushi or something," it would to be the man sitting in front of him. "I've got a can of salmon and a few potatoes left," Russell quietly offered. The woman walked up the stoop next door and rang the bell. "What's that," Tom chuckled, "Polish Sushi?" She was buzzed into the building and disappeared behind the door. "If you get us a few quarts of beer I'll make you a decent supper," Russell took off his cap, "looks like you can use it," and rubbed his forehead, "pick up some sour cream," with the palm of his left hand, "maybe some Margarine as well."

Wake up around 8, have coffee and waffles, read the funnies, do the crossword, play a few games of Solitaire, Sudoku, then nap until lunch, nap after lunch, watch television, more Solitaire or left hand vs. right hand Scrabble, have dinner, watch the local

And Then

and national news, *Wheel of Fortune, Jeopardy,* sports or sitcoms
then fall asleep on the couch around 10—nearly everyday for
two decades. I walked to the supermarket while he napped
and picked up a steak, some potatoes, and a container of mixed
greens. I brought down a strawberry cheesecake from Juniors
and a bottle of red wine. We always drank good wine together.
If I'd known this was going to be his last birthday I would've
brought more wine. Why hadn't I forced him to go to the hospital? I could have just picked him up, tossed him into the back of
an ambulance—strapped him onto the gurney and away we go.
I could have prolonged his life. Everyone who loved my father
tried to convince him to take better care of himself and now he is
gone. A few bites of steak and half a helping of mashed potatoes,
he barely touched his salad after drowning it in Ranch dressing
and only drank half a glass of wine—it was a Saint-Chinian—but
managed to eat a sizeable wedge of strawberry cheesecake and
washed that down with a tall glass of milk. I finished off the
bottle and smoked his cigarettes with the filters torn off while
we sat at the table talking and playing poker. My brother called
while we were watching *How I Met Your Mother* to wish him
happy birthday. He was 72.

When the front door closed Suzanne woke up alone on the daybed. A distant siren moved slowly along the avenue far below
the darkened windows. She pushed aside the packing blankets and placed her bare feet onto the wood floor. Her hello
echoed down the empty hall. The overhead light flickered
for a few long seconds before casting the bathroom in a cold
glow. The hissing radiator where tiny bubbles formed at the
nozzle then burst in the humid air. Her nearly dry polyester
dress and black nylon stockings were hanging over the shower
curtain rod. Suzanne puzzled over the greeting *Hello Ophelia!*
scrawled in lipstick on the tall mirror holding her disheveled
reflection.

"You boil a few medium-sized potatoes," Russell had finished cooking them, "the red ones," when Tom returned from the bodega. "Make sure you leave the skins on," Russell emptied the pot into the colander, "the flavor is in the skins," and steam rose from the sink. Tom removed two cold forties of Ballantine from the brown paper bag, "Here you go," placed one on the counter, "the sour cream and butter is in the bag." Russell cracked open the beer and took a long swallow before shaking the water off the potatoes. The wooden chair creaked beneath Tom as he sat down. Russell pulled the top off the can of salmon and a giant grey tomcat appeared in the window, "Mash them up with the fish," pushed through the torn screen then jumped onto the floor, "add a crushed pack of crackers," positioned himself at the foot of the chef, "Saltines are best," his tail flicking in anticipation, "but Ritz will work just as well." Russell jabbed each potato with the fork. "Add celery salt," dropped them back into the pot one by one, "but don't overdo it." The layout of Russell's first floor apartment appeared identical to Paula's. Tom reproached himself for drinking in the afternoon—something he hadn't done in months—wondered if there was still time to blurt out some lame excuse and leave the beer on the table—it would not go to waste—then go back upstairs to fumble through the rest of the afternoon. A long walk would help. Couldn't he just sit here and eat but not drink? The clock on the wall indicated it was nearly one. Lester Young was playing on the ancient radio atop the fridge. The walls were smeared beige with nicotine. The kitchen smelled like dank ashtray and cold coffee grounds. There was something comforting in all of this. Tom twisted off the metal cap and took a sip of beer. Russell shook the cylindrical chunk of pink fish out of the can and into the mixing bowl. "Use too much and it becomes trenchant." Tom looked up from the cat, "Trenchant?" Scraping out the leftover bits with the fork, "Celery salt will overpower everything if you aren't careful," he leaned down, "add some pepper," tapped them onto the floor, "or

And Then

Adobo." The cat set upon the morsels, "Which is mostly garlic powder and oregano with some pepper," they vanished before Russell finished saying, "the lemon flavored is best," he raised the bottle while adding, "especially for fish cakes," before taking a long pull. "Maybe chop up an onion as well, a Bermuda onion will give you the right kick." The cat crouched, "You should fry it up before mixing it in," then leapt onto the counter, "that way the onion gets crispy on the outside." Russell waved the cat away from the empty can, "Especially with cracker crumbs," who jumped on a chair then gave Tom an icy look before springing off the chair and onto the floor, "I should have told you to get an onion," he slunk down the hall as Russell asked, "Do you have one upstairs?"

Nothing, in fact, actually dies: everything goes on existing, always. No power on earth can obliterate that which has once had being. Every act, every word, every form, every thought, falls into the universal ocean of things, and produces a circle on its surface that goes on enlarging beyond the furthest bounds of eternity. The material configurations only disappear from the common gaze, while the spectres that break free from them go out to people infinity. In some unknown region of space, Paris continues to abduct Helen of Troy. Cleopatra's galley swells its silken sails on the azure blue of an ideal Cydnus. Certain impassioned and puissant spirits have always been able to call into their presence centuries that appear to have vanished into the past, and bring back to life people whom everyone knows are dead. Faust had the daughter of Tyndar for his mistress, and took her to his gothic castle, having snatched her from the mysterious gulfs of Hades. Octavian too had just lived for a day during the reign of the Emperor Titus, and had made Arria Marcella, daughter of Arrius Diomedes, fall in love with him. Now she lay beside him on an antique bed in a city that the whole world knows is destroyed.

Her purse and heels were beneath the daybed. The empty wallet held just enough change for the subway. Her coat was by the door and she pushed her arms through the sleeves before letting herself out. She rode the elevator to the marble lobby while digging in her purse for a stick of gum. A small white barking dog pulling at the end of its short leash. The doorman responded to her question by nodding toward the subway entrance at the end of the block. The D was running local and she rode it all the way down to Broadway/Lafayette.

"And it felt like a warm body pushing against you on the subway," Tom leaned forward in the chair, "like somebody sweating over you when the train pulls into the station," he removed his glasses, "Or if a person's shadow could brush against you while you were walking down the street," rubbing the bridge of his nose, "it felt like that," before putting them back on, "I just stood there while it," and the old man with the drooping mustache, "I know this doesn't make any sense," drunk on beer came back into focus, "but this shadow leaned against me."

Four months later he took a cab to the supermarket and fainted in an isle. He told me later that he was simply tired and needed to lie down. The manager called an ambulance. He spent three days in the hospital before he was released, took a cab home, made it up the stairs and collapsed on the floor. He lay on the carpet for two or maybe three days before a neighbor called to tell me the newspapers were piling up on the porch, he wasn't answering the door, or the phone. Should she call an ambulance? Would it be okay to check on him? I told her to go in and I would stay on the line. Instead she promised to call me back when she knew what was happening. I spoke to him right after she got him onto the couch, and he assured me there was nothing to worry about, I shouldn't come down, everything was going to be okay.

And Then

The black and white tiles shone in the broad patch of sunlight beneath the window facing the street. People passing in opposite directions, waiting for the bus, the silent gestures of a man talking on the pay phone, the mechanic in oil-stained blue coveralls sauntered by, a teenage couple embraced.

"I'd see her in the hall," Russell took a cigarette from the pack, "I think she was from the south," he lit it off the one burning in the ashtray, "it seemed like she had it together when she got here," stubbed out the butt, "then got mixed up with the wrong people," exhaling smoke, "and just disappeared."

I was lulled to sleep after Newark then woke up just as the train pulled into Baltimore. I could have been the only person in the car. The weird glowing vegetation that clung to the rocky embankments surrounding the empty platform before the reflection of my face was superimposed over a warehouse.

Two black salesmen in beige polyester suits strolled into the bar, greeted the bartender by his first name, apologized for being late then ordered a round of imported beers.

"All of her clothes and a new mattress," a crumpled pack of Basics, "she left everything upstairs," cigarette butts crowding the ashtray, "I remember Paula asking around," the four empty forties, "but nobody saw her again," a blue halo of smoke hanging over the table, "a few months later Paula gave me her mattress. I'm still sleeping on it." The second time they ran out of beer Tom claimed he couldn't afford to buy any more. He was as broke as Russell whose July SSI check was long gone. "I think I'm sleeping in her old room," Tom cleared his throat, "although it could have been anyone," then stood and pushed back the chair. "It was probably just wind from the storm," Russell walked him through the kitchen, "I said she disappeared," and opened the door, "not that she died. You just need to get out of that apartment more often." "To have a ghost," Tom stepped into the hall, "death is essential." Russell leaned against the doorframe, "You don't really know what you saw," with a note of contempt, "some mystery blonde walking up the stoop," thick arms crossed over his gut, "and sweating on you." Tom shrugged, "I didn't think you would understand," before walking down the hall, "but thanks for lunch." The door closed. Tom gripped the railing and began to climb the stairs.

Deserted loading docks, a staggered sequence of orange lights as the train curved through a tunnel, slipping by blocks of desolate row houses, theatrically lit graffiti adorning brick walls, running along a tall chain link fence topped with razor wire, a billboard glaring defiantly into the darkness, carried above empty intersections, through swaths of dark green, long white lights and patches of trees, flashes of suburban lawns, parking lots, illuminated vegetation glistening beneath streetlights, prefabricated condos, darkened strip malls just off the highway now adjacent to the tracks, red taillights vanishing into headlights casting onto rain-slicked roads, gas stations like small islands awash in cold fluorescents, empty intersections, darkened houses, churches, restaurants and racing over a large body of water while watching for a sign that never arrived.

Suzanne slung her purse over her shoulder before scooping the change off the bar. "I'd like to speak to detective Mike Erwin." She placed the cigarette between her lips and crossed to the phone booth. "Speaking." She pulled open the door and sat on the stool. "My grandmother asked me to call you." The booth smelled of spilled Windex. "Who is this?" She dialed the number scrawled on the matchbook before feeding all of the quarters into the slot. "This is Suzanne Johnson, my grandmother said that you had some questions for me about, *a robbery,* where

And Then

I used to work?" "Put John on the phone right now." "Who?"
"Put John on the phone...Suzanne?" "I haven't seen him since
my last day at work," she took a deep breath before adding, "I'm
not involved with any robbery," cradling the phone beneath her
ear, "and that's exactly what I told my Nana yesterday," while
pressing her knees together, "Do you think if I was I'd be calling you?" "Do you know where John is?" She tried sounding
aggressive, "What makes you think that I would have anything
to do with John?" "Because a number of employees at the supermarket said the two of you were very close." "I'm a suspect in
this nonsense because a few gossipy high school dropouts—"
"You aren't a suspect but the fact that you and John are close
isn't helping your story." She tried sounding adamant, "I had
nothing to do with that robbery," then definitive, "and I don't
know where John is." "Where are you calling from?"

Tom inserted the key in the lock. He pushed open the door and
stepped onto the frozen embankment. The woman was partially
submerged in brackish water. Facedown arms outstretched. The
door closed behind Tom as he walked over the frozen muck.
The linoleum creaked when he stepped around the log. Ankle
high waves washed over the garbage outlining the shore. While
standing before the photograph of the woman on the beach
he had the distinct impression of being watched. "And you?"
Four firemen wearing yellow hip waders secured the body to a
gurney. His face and a portion of the kitchen faintly reflected
in the glass. Tom never saw her face but someone said it was
blue and spongy—like a moldy loaf of soggy bread.

When hailing a cab outside of Union Station I learned that
drivers usually pick up two or three passengers going in
approximately the same direction before leaving the station.
Since the Metro closes at midnight and there is a shortage of
cabs I shared the ride with a chubby Delta Airlines pilot who

had been stranded at BWI due to a thunderstorm and a sleep deprived Army officer just back from Afghanistan. The officer, seated on my left, remained silent throughout the ride to Crystal City. The pilot was seated beside the driver and never stopped talking about how he had been inconvenienced by the weather. His car was in the long-term parking lot furthest away from the arrivals building at Reagan National. He drunkenly apologized for parking so far out of the way, had he known that the storm was going to cause his flight to be diverted, had he known that he was going to take the train down from BWI in the middle of the night, had he known that he would have to take this ridiculous cab ride, had he known all of that he would have parked much closer to the airport, or better yet, he would have parked at Union Station. He wouldn't shut the fuck up and when we finally reached his car he couldn't get out of the cab fast enough. I was entertaining the idea of punching him in the face then maybe stapling his lips shut for good measure until I realized that would have only prolonged this unbelievable delay.

Suzanne could claim she was anyone, "I'm at a payphone," calling from anywhere, "in a diner in Winslow," just another disembodied voice carried over a wire, "in Arizona," after feeding the phone a handful of coins. The microphone beneath his chin converted the question into signals sent through the network, "Do you have family out there?" and into the receiver she was holding to her left ear where they were reconverted into sound. She wondered if the detective was trying to stall her in order to trace the call, "I did at one time," although she knew that was impossible, "I'm sure my grandmother told you what I'm doing." "She mentioned something about you trying to track down your mother. How did you get to the bus station after your last day at work?" "My ex-boyfriend gave me a ride." "Your grandmother told me a friend from work gave you that ride." "That's what I told my grandmother because she really hates

And Then

my ex," Suzanne's confidential tone warmed in his ear, "and I'd promised her that I wasn't seeing him anymore." The detective glanced at the digital watch on his left wrist before jotting down the time of her call. "What type of car does he drive?" "A blue convertible Mustang." "Nobody at the store mentioned you getting picked up in a blue Mustang." "Because I met him in front of the 7/11." "Why there?" "I was buying cigarettes and he saw me walk out of the 7/11 when he was waiting on the light." "What's his name and where can I reach him?" "His name is Andy Data," She rested the back of her head against the wall, "he might be at his uncle's place in Sandbridge, or surfing down in Hatteras," before taking a drag off her cigarette. "Do you have his uncle's number?" "No I don't...like I said..." exhaling smoke, "we aren't all that close anymore." "I really appreciate you calling Suzanne." It sounded like he was writing everything down. "This really helps your cause and right now you need all of the help you can get." She constantly replayed the end of their conversation over in her head in the months that followed and never forgave herself for not hanging up at the end of this sentence: "My Nana was very upset when I called her yesterday, even after I told her what I just told you. Can you call her right now and tell her I had nothing to do with that robbery?" The word robbery echoed before he interjected, "Where are you staying in Winslow?" Instead she sat in the wooden booth with the phone pressed to her ear, "At a motel," in a bar on Second Avenue on a sunny Friday afternoon, "I think it's called the, uh, the Breezeway?" "You think, or that's the real name of the motel where you're staying?" Another demand, "And what's the room number?" She almost laughed at his insistence, "Why do you need to know all that?" "Don't play games with me Suzanne." She dropped the cigarette, "Seven," and crushed it beneath her shoe. "I need you to go back to that room right now and sit tight," noise in the background on his end, "I'm sending a car over to the Breezeway right now and I just need you to cooperate with

77

the officers," followed by the sound of a door slamming, "they just need to identify you and if everything checks out you'll be free to go," he lit a cigarette, "and I promise that you won't ever have to deal with me again," leaned back in his chair, "but if you aren't there, let me guarantee you something, that we are going to find you, and John," he paused then asked, "Do you understand me?" She nodded into the receiver, "Sure," before hanging up.

The woman standing next to Tom recently emigrated from Poland, she was in her early or mid-thirties, shoulder-length straight brown hair with blonde streaks, wide hazel eyes behind rectangular purple frames, arched eyebrows, dark red lips, long fingers, gold wedding band, glossy pink fingernails. Her heavily accented English was adequate. They talked about the weather then Tom mentioned a few out of the way places worth seeing during the summer—the Cloisters, Coney Island, Flushing Park, Far Rockaway—and received a lukewarm response. Had she been to the Met? Yes, she actually squeezed his forearm for emphasis, twice in one week. She, he never got her name, was nearly his height and very thin. Ten minutes later his well intentioned, naïve defense of Marxism was met with a wave of derision, as was her surprisingly lofty and equally naïve opinion of Ronald Reagan. Writing your undergraduate thesis on the Paris Commune might not make you an expert on Communism but how could anyone in their right mind believe Reagan didn't know anything about the Iran-Contra affair until after it was reported in the media? Toward the end of their pointed exchange Tom acknowledged being raised Catholic, claimed he was an Atheist, mentioned his recent experiences with the supernatural, then stated that he hadn't stepped inside a church in ten years. In turn she laughingly said that when she was young she had wanted to be a nun. The tiny gold cross and thin chain around her neck held the dim bar light. She pressed

And Then

him for details about those supposed supernatural experiences. Tom said he was cat sitting for his professor while she was in Greece for the summer and enthusiastically described the oblique shape that drifted through her kitchen during a thunderstorm then recounted his extraordinary encounter with a mysterious blonde on the stairs. The red leather purse lying open on the zinc bar held a silver money clip with a few fives and a ten, a pack of Parliaments, a box of matches and a tube of lipstick. She said her husband was at a boring business dinner or something equally dull and dismissively unspecific. Pleated knee-length black skirt, black sandals with thin leather straps wrapping around narrow ankles, symmetrical pink toenails. Would she like to go somewhere quiet where they could talk? The semi-transparent sleeveless white blouse revealed enticing views of her black bra. His haunted apartment happened to be right around the corner. The pause grew awkward when an unlikely lull in the surrounding Wednesday evening conversations accompanied a brief lapse between songs. Tom couldn't bring himself to repeat the question or further elaborate on the convenience of the nearby location and simply stood before her expectantly clutching a flat pint of watery beer. That morning he'd transcribed five pages of notes onto a borrowed word processor then rode the 6 Train up to 96th street and gradually drifted downtown. It was a hot cloudless day as people hurried past, averaging thirty determined faces per block. Those with the most deliberate strides merely paused when traffic turned into the crosswalks. The nights reading novels he pulled from Paula's shelves or wandering sweltering Manhattan sidewalks with a few dollars in his wallet grew into empty weeks. Cheap fleeting distractions only served to remind Tom that he could hardly afford to keep himself fed while writing his thesis. After a two-mile, block by block process of elimination—Chinese, pizza, hot dogs, pretzels, knishes, Vietnamese, bagels, bananas, Afghan, gyros, pastries, grilled chicken, Japanese, Greek, burgers and fries, Mexican—he finally gave into hunger in Murray Hill, inhaled two vegetarian samosas, two plates of curried chicken and roasted vegetables then got into a loud argument with the Indian waiter about which items on his bill were supposedly part of the discounted lunch menu. An hour later Tom simply nodded when the pretty cashier at the Strand asked if he wanted a bag for the three-dollar paperback he purchased with a five—which left him with ten dollars for the rest of the week. Why does it get harder to interact with people the longer you go without them? He was ridiculously broke, lonely and horny. Tom got back to the East Village and took a shower, changed into clean clothes, then walked into the bar around the corner, grimly determined to take advantage of the two-for-one happy hour. She finally responded, looking up at him from behind the rims of her purple frames, saying yes, an enticing smile revealed two rows of crowded teeth, why not, they did have enough time to leave the narrow bar that was just around the corner from his haunted apartment, okay, let's climb four flights of stairs and continue our conversation without having to compete with this continuous barrage of industrial techno. The old drunk on the stoop slurred something obscene that she didn't understand although his accompanying gesture had universal significance. Tom fixed her a tall screwdriver, apologized for not having any ice, adding that the vodka had been in the freezer for at least a month. She claimed they didn't have very much time and promptly drank half of it while standing before the kitchen counter. He chanced a quick kiss on her cheek. The spray of honeyed perfume lingering behind her ears reminded him of pollen-dusted bees. Her mouth tasted like vodka and cigarettes. She helped him undo the buttons on her blouse and bra clasp. His fingers covered a constellation of reddish freckles. Her small brown nipples were already hard. She closed her eyes when they kissed, embraced, and kissed before moving toward the front room. He kicked off his sneakers in the doorway and she pulled

And Then

off his T-shirt. Two pairs of glasses clattered off the stack of splayed paperbacks and onto the floor. She dropped the top then stepped out of the skirt, shed the beige cotton panties but left her sandals on. It took him a long minute to find the condoms without his glasses, naked and blushing in the curtained sunset, yet he denied being nervous. She slowly unrolled one over his erection then rode him with her eyes closed, purposefully grinding away, rubbing her clitoris with two then four fingers. He watched in disbelief as she reached a quick climax—felt it flutter through her pelvis—then gripped her waist with both hands and fucked her like he wanted to take her orgasm back. She came again just before he did.

I asked the driver stop at the 7/11 closest to my father's place so I could get cash out of the ATM to pay for the ride. It was two-thirty in the morning when I finally pushed open the door and climbed the stairs. My father was lying on his back between the couch and the coffee table. He had fallen while attempting to answer the phone. He was soaked in piss and shit. I picked him up and got him onto the couch, assuring him that I was there, and that everything was going to be okay. Would he like a glass of water? Yes. A cigarette? No. Would he like to take a shower and change his clothes? No.

Suzanne took a final drag off the cigarette, "His helicopter was shot down," then crushed it in the ashtray, "but he saved a few people before he died so they gave him the Purple Heart." Nick drew the brown liquid off the blackened spoon, "How old were you?" through the tiny clump of cotton and into the syringe. "I was seven." "He was a pilot?" "An advisor," Suzanne shook her head, "Some fishermen found his body." "And your mom," Nick fingered the vein in the crook of her left arm, "what's the story there?" "My mother left me after that," Suzanne winced, "like a few days after the funeral," then Nick pulled the belt off

81

her arm, "she left me with her parents." He could taste her rush while watching the heroin wash over her. "So you were raised by your grandparents?" The second side of Bowie's *Hunky Dory* was playing quietly on the portable turntable. "I never saw my mom again." A gust of snow covered the window overlooking the darkened block. "I guess she couldn't deal with me," her eyes softened, "so in a way," as she contemplated the black kitten sleeping on the pillow, "they both died in Vietnam." "You must remember them," Nick sounded very far away, "that's something," although he was right beside her cooking up his hit. Suzanne lay back on the mattress, "I have memories of them," and closed her eyes, "but they aren't very useful."

She was already dressed when Tom joined her in the kitchen. "You know something strange?" Looking somehow older yet more beautiful as she lit a cigarette off the stove. Handing over her glasses, "What's that?" She put them on before saying, "My husband is a friend with that photographer." "What photographer?" Pointing at the color photograph of the blonde on the beach, "That's a Brian Kimble," hanging beside the telephone, "You don't know him?"

Sitting at the table with the phone and canceling his accounts. Deep cracks ran along the ceiling and down the walls. Keying through automated prompts then explaining to customer service representatives that my father had a medical emergency and was lucky to be alive. Thick beige carpet, both couches faced the darkened television, a wicker rocking chair. "When he gets out of the hospital we've arranged for him to be transferred to a rehab facility in Charlottesville, near my younger brother, and after his release, he's going to live with my brother and his family, so no, let's just go ahead and cancel the account." The dusty glass coffee tabletop ringed by beer bottles. "We're going to renovate his townhouse and then sell it." Both couches were

And Then

fouled with urine and grime. Spider webs suspended before the casement windows. The woman at the *Washington Post* said they processed his order for Monday so a final copy of the paper would be delivered in the morning. Their silken egg sacs were clustered in the metal frames. A ceremonial officers sword mounted to a slab of varnished wood hung on the wall opposite the television. He was paid up for the quarter so they would mail a refund in a few weeks. Everything stained some nicotine shade of beige. Where should she send the check? The portable blue cassette radio was shaped like a small pod. The man at the power company convinced me to suspend the account otherwise I would have to open a new one when the renovations began which would cost more and take longer than reactivating his account. He never listened to the radio and didn't own any cassettes. Arrangements were made for his bills to be sent to my brother's address. I smacked it on the back, like a doctor delivering a baby, and that got the radio to work. Most of the casement windows had been pried open. Dappled sunlight played off the leaves. I never told anyone that afternoon how much I loved my father although I'd been drinking on an empty stomach since returning from the hospital. The radio was on top of the broken air conditioner beneath a window in the living room. Shadows of branches appeared on the walls when clouds drifted away from the sun. The occasional call of a blue jay. WETA was playing a lot of Brahms that weekend in celebration of his 177th birthday. Pine branches hung over the couches. The lamp and side table were bathed in afternoon sunlight. Squirrels occasionally nested in the attic and were usually evicted after birthing litters among the piles of junk. An elegant magnolia grew up right outside the kitchen table. House sparrows would light on the windowsills then peek inside, their heads cocked in curiosity, the way a visitor at the zoo might pause before their own silhouette in the darkened window display of a tree dwelling marsupial. The last call

I made was to Bell Atlantic and they shut off his phone a few hours later.

Nick dreamt of the insect city where he was perched atop an anthill—clumps of dirt, twigs and pebbles dominated the fore-ground—as human figures strolled high above the grass sky-line. Occasional voices alternated with the flitting buzz of flying ants. He woke up in the dark while intermittent waves of traffic slowly moved along the slush-covered street.

The breeze from the box fan in the window cooled the sweat on Tom's forehead and bare chest, "That's not mine," picking up her glass, "this is my professor's place," which was damp, "I'm just here for the summer," and when he drank from it, "but no," condensation trailed down his left wrist, "I don't know his work." Olive jumped onto the kitchen table to get a better look at her. "You're serious?" She sounded surprised, "that's an early one," exhaling smoke, "what a pretty cat," then added a few lines in Polish that neither Tom nor the cat understood. Olive sat back on her haunches and began licking her belly. "He has a show right now in Soho," taking a drag off her cigarette before suggesting, "you should go see it." Tom sounded indifferent, "I'm not really into art," while thinking of the prints and contact sheets he'd found in one of the boxes that Paula had asked him to throw away, "But is that worth a lot of money?" She nodded, "Everything sold at the opening," then noticed the clock on the wall, "I have to leave." It was seven-thirty. "Maybe we have time for another—" "No," Shaking her head, "I have to go back," and touched by his disappointment, "to where my husband is meeting me." Tom sighed, "That was really nice." "Yes," she gathered her purse from the counter, "but I didn't get to meet your ghost." He followed her to the door, "Maybe next time," and watched her descend a flight of stairs. When she didn't look back he closed the door. Tom crossed the kitchen, realized he

And Then

didn't even get her name, and examined the lipstick on the rim of the glass. Olive jumped onto the counter. "Do *you* want to know something strange?" Tom caressed her behind the ears before saying, "That was the best sex I've ever had."

I bagged up the bottles on the counter and put the bag on the floor beside the trashcan before opening the fridge to get another beer. The kale in the crisper drawer and half-eaten package of seitan on the top shelf were my sister's leftovers. She flew out from San Francisco two weeks ago and spent a week facilitating his homecare attendant visits, cooking for him, bathing him, then called an ambulance when he had to go back to the hospital. I took a train down from Penn Station the morning he was admitted. My sister and I met up outside the ICU that afternoon. DNR was stamped on his chart. My mother drove up from Richmond to lend her support. The doctors were cautiously optimistic—he was gradually stabilizing—my sister saved his life. They kept him in the ICU for one more day before he was transferred to a room on the 11th floor. My sister and I spent the rest of the week at his bedside as he regained a bit of personality while undergoing a battery of tests and procedures. I hired a lawyer to come in and they drafted up his will. Why not wait until the very last minute? They made me the executor. A long-term care administrator found a rehab facility in Charlottesville that accepted his insurance. My brother and his family arrived on Friday afternoon then spent the weekend at the hospital. My sister flew back to San Francisco on Sunday. My mother agreed to drive up from Richmond on Tuesday morning and take him to Charlottesville. I had to oversee one more procedure, sign off on his release, and close up the townhouse.

Nick's reoccurring dream of getting busted by the fat mustached cop: Instead of being hauled off to the precinct where this narrative frequently unfurled, Nick gets shoved into the back of a cab and driven out to Queens. The cop introduced Nick to his wife, a skinny blonde with a black eye, desperate to have a baby. In a matter-of-fact tone the cop advises Nick that if he is going to continue shooting dope like the A-bomb is on its way then he should seriously consider acquiring a more reliable income stream. The three of them are standing around in ankle deep brown shag with black light posters and macramé owls adorning the walls. Burning candles, an open tub of Vaseline that doubled as an ashtray, a menagerie of knives, tall glass water pipes and mirrors cluttered the marble altar beside the waterbed. The dream cop's wife tells him to relax while exhaling a cloud of smoke from a long blue cigarette. Nick watches himself undress then wakes up after a door in the building slams.

Tom woke up with a headache. A loud argument running along the block escalated from shouted curses to thrown bottles and abruptly ended with four rapid pops that must have been gun-shots. He knocked the box of Q-tips into the sink while root-ing through the cabinet for aspirin. Alternating sirens rapidly approaching from opposite directions indicated that the police and an ambulance were on the way. He swallowed two tablets with a palm-full of warm tap water then caught a glimpse of his bleary-eyed self in the mirror. Pulsating red and blue lights saturated the ceiling. He lay down on the futon and waited for the throbbing between his temples to subside. Static punctu-ated numerical commands from police radios filled the humid air. The wooden chair before the desk appeared animated in the fluctuating glow. EMS personnel loaded the gunshot vic-tim into an idling ambulance. He couldn't see the desk clock, couldn't be bothered with putting on his glasses and assumed it was between four and five. A door slammed before the diesel engine was finally shifted into drive. He thought of the aspirin dissolving in his stomach while clutching a feather pillow in his arms. Tom drifted off alternately wondering if the shooting

And Then

would be in the news and how his body knew exactly where to send the pain relief.

The shelves that once held my books now contained an incomplete set of Time Life home repair manuals, a Rand McNally World Atlas, photo albums, stacks of board games, Naval citations, college yearbooks, Scrabble dictionaries, a clear plastic bag full of red, white, and blue poker chips, the crumbling paperback copy of Ed McBain's *Bread* that I'd written a book report about in the 7th grade. The living room was reflected in the dusty television screen. When I lived with my father the stereo was beside the television. Rows of albums and wooden fruit crates crammed with cassettes filled the space below. Two tall speakers faced the living room. If today had been a weekday afternoon in the spring of '86 and I'd just come home from school every wave of distortion on The Jesus and Mary Chain's *Psychocandy* would be ripping through this townhouse. An imitation brass wall relief of a clipper ship surrounded by rough waves hung above the television. Cobwebs dangling from the ceiling were caught up in the sails.

A frigid draft pressed upon the coats and blankets. Nick recalled being dressed when they got high. Suzanne had removed his sneakers but left on his socks. His feet were toasty warm. The bulky layers they lay beneath made him think that in a few centuries a team of bespectacled archeologists in pith hats and khaki uniforms would gradually unearth this room and eventually brush all the dirt away from their grinning skulls. When Nick nudged Suzanne she stopped snoring. He fell asleep listening to the intimate yet distant sound of heels moving along the narrow path cleared through the ice and snow.

Brian recognized his handwriting, "Do you want money," on the manila envelope, "is that why you're here?" Tom was seated on the edge of the black couch, "No I just," in a colossal loft, "I'm completely broke," with his back to a row of open windows, "but that's not why I'm here," eight stories above Canal Street on a hot Wednesday afternoon, "to be honest I really hadn't thought of that." Brian undid the metal clasp and removed the pictures, "Where did you get these?" It took Tom an entire afternoon to find the gallery, "They were in these boxes that I was asked to throw away," and a few days after showing the owner what he had, "when I opened one of them I found these pictures," he received a call from the gallery informing him that Brian Kimble would like to meet with him at his loft tomorrow afternoon. "Where were they?" Tom cleared his throat before saying, "I'm cat sitting at my professor's place for the summer," then pressed his palms on the knees of his jeans, "Professor Avloniti?" "Paula," Brian attempted to smile, "They were in her apartment?" Tom nodded, "Along with some records and clothes. But I didn't know who you were or that they might be worth anything."

We met at a new wave dance club in Georgetown. It was a Saturday night in April of '85 and her birthday. She was there with her mother, who was acting as chaperone, and a few girlfriends. I was there with my fake ID and the girl from William and Mary that I'd lost my virginity to the previous summer. We danced together a lot (the girl from William and Mary claimed she didn't care although we never saw each other after that night) then while she was leaving I followed her outside and got her name and number. She is named after the month of her birth and shares her birth-date with Billie Holiday. We spent hours on the phone the following afternoon. I was still living with my mother in Virginia Beach and just visiting with my brother and sister over the break. She lived with her mother in Reston. Her father was in NYC or somewhere out on Long Island and they rarely saw each other. It was easy to make her laugh and she

And Then

was really funny. We liked a lot of the same bands although she reluctantly confessed to occasionally listening to Duran Duran. Our conversation was spontaneous and intimate as I sat on the kitchen floor with the receiver pressed to my ear. She was really pretty although the club had been very dark. I couldn't remember the color of her eyes but kept that to myself. She was very intelligent and sounded so sophisticated. We spoke until both of my ears ached. I finally had to say goodbye after my father yelled at me to get off the phone.

The dream cop's wife assures Nick that her husband brings home a different man to fuck her almost every night, that he used to sit in the closet and watch, when it turned him on, but now he just goes down to the bar and watches football. She really likes sucking his cock—nearly swallowing him while cupping his balls with both hands—but it feels like a numb flesh-colored balloon. Is he too afraid to get it up? She is wearing a black garbage bag so they won't stain the sheets. Telling him to relax while lifting the bag like a shinny rubber umbrella to reveal her shapely waist and spreading her cream-colored thighs while demanding that he get her off. He dutifully fingers her hairy pussy and asshole until she has an orgasm. Nick wakes up with an erection—recalling her damp elasticity while examining his hands in the dim light. How real it felt to slowly wedge his fingers inside the dream cop's wife.

Brian regarded the picture of Suzanne looking pensive in the back of a cab. He just told her that he was in love with her, in spite of all her bullshit, and they should be living together, or was that the night he discovered the tracks running out of the crook of her left arm? Either way she freaked out on him again because he just couldn't be bothered to acknowledge her forever-changing boundaries. Whenever they went to clubs or shows she would be surrounded by a half-dozen strivers the minute he turned his back—complimenting her hair and clothes—wanting to dance with her or share their drugs or get her number if only that tool on her arm would take a fucking hike. He would fend them off as best he could then spend the rest of the night trying to reconnect without being, *a hypersensitive-possessive-chauvinist-pig* about it, or risk losing her to the most aggressive clown in the jostling circle of tweaked suitors. Her heavy heroin use was truly the end of them. Rumor had it she married a stockbroker and was living in the Hamptons. Brian never knew that Suzanne died from an overdose and that her body had been dumped in the East River.

I shared every significant experience with my father. Each passion, success, failure, ambition and frustration passed through his townhouse. Every episode, which comprised my late teens, twenties and thirties, decades of poverty I embraced while editing and writing, was sounded out at his table. Low paying jobs and failed relationships carried me back here, as my obsessions gradually became manuscripts, which were eventually published. The less I fretted over his health the closer we became.

A final drag off the cigarette, "You always take forever coming back," she crushed in the ashtray, "that's why I want to go with you." Nick drew the brown liquid through the tiny clump of cotton, "Because you don't trust me," and into the syringe. "I totally trust you." Coffee cups with crystallized clumps of mud colored sugar stuck inside them, "I'll always come back," empty packs of Marlboros, matchbooks and candy wrappers littered the floor. "Yeah," Suzanne nodded, "for my money," and looked into his eyes. "This is just enough for your wake up," Nick picked at the flaking scab on her right ankle, "and then we'll both go." They had serious discussions about quitting after Christmas or maybe Valentine's Day. "You say that but you always go without me." He withdrew the needle and watched the laconic calm

find her face. "I always come back with sweets for the sweet."
Two broad columns of smoke suspended above the mattress.
"Because of my money." Wind rattled the windows. "And when
that's gone you'll be out that door." Nick was hunkered down
in a windowless cement bunker with damp walls. "Don't be
like that honey pot." Orange light outlined the doorframe and
when he pushed down on the metal bar the door swung open.
He stepped into baking sunlight as the door slammed behind
him. There was no handle on the grey metal door and he'd left
his works inside the squat windowless cement building in the
middle of nowhere—no trees, or grass, or sand—from here to
the dusty orange horizon. He circled the building and the door
was gone. Nick hoisted himself onto the roof and that crum-
bled into the mattress. Suzanne lay beside him, "Shellfish," and
closed her eyes. He snorted, "What?" "You're like a clam or a
real skinny lobster."

Brian set the images on the coffee table beside a pack of unfil-
tered Camels and a chrome Zippo. "She was my . . . Suzanne was
Paula's roommate." "Do you know what happened to her?" Brian
shrugged, "She started using heroin," scratched the stubble on
his chin, "this was twelve years ago," looked blankly at the young
man across from him, "then just vanished," and sighed, "but we
weren't really close by the time that happened."

The next day I forced my brother and sister onto a bus that we
rode all the way out to Tysons Corner because they were too
young to be left alone all afternoon. A pretty brunette with an
asymmetrical bob and dark brown eyes was standing by the curb
when we finally got there. And now those hours are a blur of
shimmering images. What did we talk about? I don't remember
kissing her but just before saying goodbye she sprayed her favorite perfume (Paloma Picasso) on the cuffs of my mustard yellow
cardigan. That cardigan belonged to my grandfather and I still

Donald Breckenridge

wear it although now it is full of holes. I couldn't wait for the spring semester to end so I could see her again. We were inseparable during the summer and ecstatic when I moved in with my father just before school began in September. We remained a couple for seven years. I followed her to Brooklyn and we lived together on Lafayette Avenue while she studied photography. She was my formative first love and we gave freely to each other until my infidelities eventually destroyed our relationship. I left her in the spring of '92 to travel through Europe with my soon to be first wife, an Austrian painter, and we married in Brooklyn that August. I left her in the fall of '97 to have a long affair with a Polish nuclear engineer who was eleven years older than I was and raising her two children in Carmel, NY. A few years later I met a pretty writer at a party and she would eventually become my second wife.

They walked through the falling snow with their heads down. "Some creature that tastes good but isn't very smart." A city bus had stalled near the corner. "Lobsters are noble." The driver was sitting alone in a passenger seat. A giant tow truck was blocking the traffic. "They might be but they aren't very bright." They stood on the corner and when the light changed they crossed the street. Nick had his hands jammed in the front pockets of his jeans. Two Chinese children were peering out at them from the watery patches in the window of the takeout restaurant. "I can't help being honest." He hocked up a mouthful of phlegm and spit into the wind. Three hooded figures huddled around a burning garbage can. Nick walked up a stoop and Suzanne followed him. He rang the bell and then they waited.

Tom was on the landing unlocking the door to Paula's apartment when the wooden steps creaked as if someone was walking up the stairs. He turned around and immediately recognized the blonde from the photographs. She was dressed in a long black coat and carrying a black umbrella in her right hand. He didn't have time to step out of the way or even be afraid. A cold breeze carried her energy and when that entered his chest it coursed through every cell. It was a vibrantly white sensation that caused the hair on the back of his head to stand on end. Tom never forgot the feeling or tired of telling the story—she just walked right through him.

Suzanne lost count after five, or maybe six, consecutive days of snow before it turned into steady rain. Thursday through Monday, or maybe it was Wednesday when this shit began in earnest. The illuminated blue clock on the wall of the dry cleaners indicated that it was only seven, although the empty sidewalks and infrequent traffic made it seem much later. Was it still Monday? Red and yellow neon melted the snow into shallow puddles. She thought of the blue skies and sandy beaches found in the glossy pages of travel magazines. Suzanne removed her keys while climbing the stoop and unlocked the door. What if this metal door opened onto an impossibly bright and beautiful sandy beach? Turquoise waves quietly washed upon a pristine shore as warm ocean breezes scented with tropical blossoms carried the calls of exotic birds. When Suzanne closed the umbrella cold water splashed onto her left wrist. She stepped around bundles of soaked newspaper then slowly climbed the flights of filthy stairs. Suzanne dropped the umbrella by the mat then turned the keys in their locks before pushing open the door.

And Then

I set the table as the album ended. A letter from my girlfriend arrived that afternoon. My camera was on the table beside a yellow processing envelope filled with color photographs. The tone arm lifted the needle away from the record, swung over the vinyl and dropped onto the holder before the turntable clicked off. She went to Australia in January as a foreign exchange stu-

Donald Breckenridge

dent and would not return until mid-June. A part-time job at a neighborhood camera store enabled me to afford my growing interest in photography. We wrote to each other nearly everyday; those letters took seven days to cross the world and contained minute updates on the excruciatingly slow passing of time, earnest declarations of fidelity and everlasting love. The water was nearing a boil, spaghetti sauce bubbled in another pot, garlic bread warmed in the oven. I paraphrased song lyrics in many of my letters, copied out passages from books and included some of my earliest attempts at photography—images of garbage I'd hunt down along the banks of a nearby runoff stream—which captured my alienation and crushing loneliness. My father stopped in at a hotel bar near his office every evening for a few gin martinis before driving home. The yellow envelope contained twenty-four pictures of a smashed reel-to-reel tape recorder I'd discovered in a tall clump of weeds then hauled up an embankment and tossed onto a concrete causeway. He would return between five and seven-thirty and was progressively tanked by the end of the workweek. We frequently argued politics while watching the evening news. The fact that I passionately hated Ronald Reagan, was a vegetarian, and an animal rights activist who had registered for the selective service as a conscientious objector got him riled up, but all of my anarcho peace punk bluster never really bothered him because he knew I was earnest. He was baffled by many of my opinions, bemused by my politics and while he remained a staunch conservative throughout his life, those long arguments as the CBS evening news played out before us were nearly always civil. I never convinced him that the Republican Party was inherently evil, that US and Soviet imperialism represented the greatest threat to all life on the planet, eating animals was barbaric, or that smoking three packs of cigarettes a day would eventually kill him, and yet, we were a lot like a pair of reluctant bachelors living under the same roof who happened to enjoy each oth-

94

er's company. He was the furthest thing from a disciplinarian. I liked cooking for him on the evenings when I wasn't working, so dinner was usually on the table when he came home. He was a mellow drinker and frequently fell asleep on the couch after eating. I'd read at the table or do my homework as game shows segued into sports or sitcoms. After packing himself off to bed I might load up my Walkman and go for a long walk or take his car into DC and see a band but most nights I just played the stereo while writing letters or reading until I fell asleep on the couch. I lived with my father for nearly a year before he bought me a bed.

The three windows in the bedroom never provided enough sunlight even with the curtains pulled back and the shades wound up. He abandoned his double bed for the couches in the living room a decade ago. The top of the dresser was covered with piles of change, eyeglasses, packages of eye patches, a few rolls of quarters, the brass lamp with the brittle white shade, empty contact lens holders, bottles of lens wash, a ceramic beer mug overflowing with coins, balled up pairs of mismatched socks. A dusty mirror affixed to the dresser held up a tall portion of the cluttered room.

In his bed I spun long sensible lists into nothing. All the things I would convince him to do, not just to stay alive but so he could enjoy his life, backed by selfless arguments for why he should heed my advice. Ill-fitting threadbare sheets, a tangle of cotton blankets, two foam pillows encased in blue flannel. My fear that he would die on the couch while I slept in his bed always overtook me. All the time I spent with him was simply facilitating his death—the obedient eldest son putting on a good show by washing the dishes, doing the shopping and taking care of the laundry once or twice a month—I might have begged him to see a doctor but I could never force him to save his own life. Instead

Donald Breckenridge

I bought cartons of cigarettes and packages of candy bars so he wouldn't have to leave his house. I was a compliant witness during this slow suicide and a principal enabler. I would get out of bed, regardless of how much alcohol I might have consumed, to stand in the living room and turn on the overhead light while listening for a faint rasping breath. Now that he is gone, I frequently think of how reassuring it was to watch him, horribly frail in the dim light, snoring into oblivion on that filthy couch where he spent so many years simply waiting to die.

The windows were either wide open or cracked a bit depending on the season and provided at least a portion of breathable air. The traffic running along 395 grew dim after midnight then louder before rush hour, droning air conditioners, rising and falling sirens. My self-delusion always peaked a few hours before dawn. Occasional helicopters. The downstairs neighbors—entertaining or watching television—muffled by the floor. A chorus of house sparrows announcing every morning accompanied by crow calls, jay, robin, and cardinal songs. The hydraulic breaks on a city bus slowing for speed bumps, and then finally, the muffled footfalls of the paperboy followed by the dull thud of the newspaper hitting the small cement porch beneath the bedroom windows always sent me back to sleep.

The heavy wooden desk buried beneath piles of unopened junk mail, birthday and Christmas cards, a semi-transparent plastic shopping bag filled with empty cardboard boxes, a forever blinking digital alarm clock, spent ballpoint pens, piles of pennies and paid bills, grocery circulars, expired coupon booklets for shuttered businesses, the open package of blank Hallmark Christmas cards and dark green envelopes, random outdoor sporting catalogs, community newsletters, a beige coffee mug doubling as an ashtray, a muddled glass ashtray, empty disposable lighters, owners manuals for the car, toaster, and television.

And Then

The drawers contained a jumble of colorful chest ribbons and medals, citations, generic-looking eyeglasses with thick lenses, business cards from former colleagues at defunct corporations, road maps, an empty box of tissues, dismantled mechanical pens, a shattered compass, decades-old optometrists appointment cards, spent ballpoint pens, empty flint dispensers, expired security passes where each small square color photo captured his warmly passive half-smile, a dismantled chrome Zippo, nearly empty metro cards illustrated with pandas or national monuments, contact lens holders, random house keys.

The desk was surrounded on three sides by tall piles of paper, the box for the toaster we purchased together at a local Best Buy a few years ago held the broken toaster it replaced, at least five years worth of cable bills, a half-melted plastic garbage can smeared with ashes, a broken black umbrella. Two large boxes filled with bank statements and cancelled checks dating back to when he opened a checking account at a local Arlington bank which was acquired by a regional bank then taken over by a national bank and finally absorbed by an international bank that was bailed out by the federal government to avoid defaulting on billions of dollars worth of debt. Credit card and credit union statements strewn along the Oriental carpet interspersed with annual shareholder statements and quarterly notices from a multinational aerospace manufacturer.

The narrow bed covered in bath towels and piles of laundered sheets. A flesh colored mattress and box spring set upon a metal frame affixed to four small wheels. My old bed still rolled. I sat down on the towels and rested my elbows on my knees. Although it would be hard to leave this home, we had saved his life, so everything was going to work itself out. I was reflected in the dusty bedroom mirror across all of this clutter at my delusional best.

Donald Breckenridge

I arrived at the hospital on the morning of his discharge with the suitcase my sister packed for him. He was able to feed himself again, with supervision, but his teeth hadn't been brushed in weeks. I thickened a cup of water, so he wouldn't choke while I brushed his teeth, and playing the clown, I added enough thickener so the toothbrush stood upright in the center of the clear plastic cup. When the nurse went off to find a wheelchair, I told him I knew he wanted to die at home and I respected his choice but we were not yet ready to say goodbye. His expression softened as my words registered, then he looked up and thanked me.

My mother pulled up as the nurse wheeled my father over to the curb. I opened the passenger door and said hello while arranging a few towels on the seat. When I said goodbye my father slipped two fingers through a hole in the quilt on his lap and wiggled them around while telling me not to cry. The nurse got him into the car then my parents drove away. That was the last time I spoke to my father. I last saw him in early August when he was back in the hospital—semi-coherent and in a great deal of pain. The infection in his head went misdiagnosed for too long and the doctors were baffled by what was causing his seizures. Once his condition stabilized he was discharged from the hospital and sent to a rehab facility where his health deteriorated to the point where he was sent back to the hospital, then to rehab, then to the hospital, then to a hospice. He died in September.

As I-95 winds though South Philadelphia it passes by the Navy Yard. From the bus you can glimpse the cluster of vacant row houses where we lived in the early Seventies. After my father returned from Vietnam he was stationed in Rhode Island, although I have no concrete memories of living there, before we moved to Philadelphia. The base housing was teaming with children and nearly all my memories of living there are idyllic.

And Then

Those row houses were very small, especially for so many young families, but there was plenty of space to play outdoors. Packs of kids were outside from morning till night on the weekends and during summer. I roamed around all summer in shorts with no shirt or shoes. My skin turned dark brown and the soles of my feet were little pads of leather by the time school began. My father built me a wooden scooter that took me everywhere. I remember the grinding sound the small metal wheels made while racing along the concrete, the rhythmic clicks while bounding over the creased sidewalks as lines of parked cars, fire hydrants and strips of green grass sailed by. I wore down the tall front tire on a Big Wheel in that neighborhood and learned how to ride a bike there as well. My father built kites that he taught me to fly in a large empty lot behind the houses. Planes making their final approach to the airport would come in low and directly overhead although I never flew my kites quite high enough to reach them. One afternoon he presented me with a boomerang. It was hard solid plastic, either red or orange, with instructions embossed on the underside. I studied the illustrations then got my grip on the handle exactly right before hurling it out into the empty lot. To my amazement the boomerang flew in a perfect arc and came whirling back. I was too surprised to catch it or even step out of the way. It smacked me on the forehead. I began howling in pain as I ran home in tears. I followed the instructions, even got it right on the first try, yet the results completely overwhelmed me. My father promptly confiscated the boomerang and I never saw it again.

He talked about his own death constantly, "I'm leaving you enough money to bury me," how tired he was of living, "and there should be a little left over for you kids as well," never missing an opportunity to compare his withered body with the broken appliances, "once I'm gone," and piles of filth surrounding him. "We might not be going anywhere when we die,"

Donald Breckenridge

I told him about the woman who lived above me, "maybe our souls linger in the worst possible places," who took her own life, "maybe we just linger in the location of our misery," and how he shouldn't be in such a hurry to leave, "because I don't think she got very far." She was an unemployed journalist suffering from a serious bi-polar disorder, "When her health insurance and unemployment ran out," an intelligent and articulate black woman in her early-thirties, "she tried to maintain some semblance of normalcy by self-medicating with alcohol." We usually exchanged a friendly if superficial hello, "While burning through her savings and maxing out her credit cards," whenever we saw each other on the stairs. She lived above me for about three years, "Her beer and liquor bottles usually filled the recycling bin," although I never got to know her. "Late one weeknight she left the building and walked over to the nearby subway station," I didn't find out about what happened, "then took off all her clothes on the platform," until a few days later, "climbed down onto the tracks and walked into the tunnel," when I overheard one of her roommates telling the mailman that she killed herself, "an oncoming train struck and killed her instantly." When I lived there I spent nearly all of my time writing. "A week after she died I woke up really late and I had to pee." My room had a separate entrance from the rest of the 2nd floor so I rarely saw my roommates. "I pulled on a pair of shorts and pocketed my keys." To use the bathroom or kitchen I had to cross the landing and unlock a dead bolted door. "I walked down the hall and went to the bathroom." The building was completely silent, "I left the bathroom," a dim circular overhead fluorescent, "and stepped out into the hall," the smell of industrial disinfectant, "the stairwell creaked as if someone was coming down the stairs," the gouged yellow wall and loose black banister, "and then this warm breeze enveloped me," two red metal doors at opposite ends of the landing, "this pure white, like, mentholated energy, passed right through me." He looked

And Then

up from the hand I dealt him and shook his head. We had this conversation, "I know it was her," a month after I encountered the ghost on the stairs. Slapping my palms on the kitchen table, "I was completely sober." A cigarette was burning in the ashtray. "Her spirit passed right through me." Smoke hung above us in late afternoon sunlight. "My hair stood up on end and it stayed like that for the rest of the night." A warm spring afternoon four years before he died. "I'm completely serious, I got back to my room completely charged with energy, charged with her energy, and I couldn't fall asleep." The windows were open. "It was incredible." Birdsongs mingled with a distant siren. I picked up my cards then took two from the hand and placed them facedown on the table.

Two weeks after my father's funeral I went back to Alexandria to meet with the estate lawyer, clean out his townhouse and hire a contactor to do the renovations. On Friday night I was able to drink myself to sleep but that didn't work Saturday night. The people I'd hired to haul everything away agreed to get there before nine on Sunday morning but I didn't fall asleep until dawn. In the dream my father and I were sitting in the living room. It seemed like the beginning of a typical visit except he had both of his eyes and a bright green aura about him. I was very happy to see him. We sat together catching up on the events that transpired since my last visit—like his death and the funeral. Later we reminisced about what an absentminded kid I had been and we both laughed as I recalled the time with the boomerang, when we were living in Philadelphia. Did he remember that? Yes, he remembered, he had been there, and then he added that he would always be there. I woke up with a jolt and realized I'd overslept. A large truck came to a stop outside. A few doors slammed followed by approaching foot-falls. I really wanted to cry but I couldn't. It took them about forty-five minutes to haul everything away.

A few terrific people helped me usher *And Then* into existence—namely my wife and courageous first reader Johannah Rodgers, Ted Pelton saw the potential in early drafts then encouraged me to develop the manuscript well beyond my own initial expectations, Eugene Lim, Jeremy M. Davies, and the gracious Chelsea Bingham for their remarkable support and enthusiasm, Derek Debevic for his thirty-years of friendship and for never accepting any money for gas while ferrying me through the wilds of obligation and living memory in Northern Virginia, Douglas Glover who published extracts of *And Then* in *Numéro Cinq* and who wrote the introduction, and finally Monica de la Torre and Betsy Sussler for publishing a lengthy extract from *And Then* in *BOMB*.

Sibylle Plogstedt's autobiographical essay *Political Repression: Moves Against the Left in West Germany* (*Critique* Vol.6 1976) was tremendously valuable in helping me shape a portion of this manuscript, as was the *NAVMC 2616, Unit Leaders Personal Response Handbook* (Department of the Navy 1967). The paragraph taken from Richard Holmes' translation of Théophile Gautier's short story *The Tourist* from the collection *My Fantoms* (*NYRB* © 1976, 2008) was used with kind permission from Richard Holmes and Edwin Frank at NYRB Classics.

Harris County Public Library
Houston, Texas

DONALD BRECKENRIDGE lives in Brooklyn with his spouse, Johannah Rodgers. He is the Fiction Editor of the Brooklyn Rail, Co-Founder and Co-Editor of In Translation, and the Managing Editor of Red Dust Books. This is his fourth novel.

DOUGLAS GLOVER has published four novels, five story collections, and three works of nonfiction. In 2003 he won the Governor-General's Award for Fiction, and in 2005 he was a finalist for the International IMPAC Dublin Literary Award. His most recent book is *Savage Love* (2013). He currently teaches writing at Vermont College of Fine Arts and edits the online literary magazine *Numéro Cinq*.